Y0-CBJ-273

Tales From Moominvalley

Other Avon Camelot Books by
Tove Jansson

COMET IN MOOMINLAND	26229	$1.25
FINN FAMILY MOOMINTROLL	25692	$1.25
MOOMINLAND MIDWINTER	30205	$1.25
MOOMINPAPPA AT SEA	34157	$1.25
MOOMINSUMMER MADNESS	28522	$1.25
MOOMINVALLEY IN NOVEMBER	30544	$1.25
THE EXPLOITS OF MOOMINPAPPA	37390	$1.25

TOVE JANSSON was born in Helsingfors, Finland, and grew up in a household full of books. She became a painter as an adult and studied art in Finland, Sweden, and France. She began writing for children as play, something apart from her serious work, and still creates children's books out of an enjoyment of fantasy. Ms. Jansson was awarded the Hans Christian Andersen International Medal for her Moomin books.

Tales From Moominvalley

Written and Illustrated by
TOVE JANSSON

Translated by **THOMAS WARBURTON**

AN AVON CAMELOT BOOK

AVON BOOKS
A division of
The Hearst Corporation
959 Eighth Avenue
New York, New York 10019

Copyright © 1963 by Tove Jansson.
English translation copyright © 1963
by Ernest Benn Limited.
Published by arrangement with Henry Z. Walck, Inc.
ISBN: 0-380-31773-7

All rights reserved, which includes the right
to reproduce this book or portions thereof in
any form whatsoever. For information address
Henry Z. Walck, Inc., Division of David McKay Co., Inc.,
750 Third Avenue, New York, New York 10017

First Camelot Printing, February, 1977
Third Printing

CAMELOT TRADEMARK REG. U.S. PAT. OFF. AND IN
OTHER COUNTRIES, MARCA REGISTRADA, HECHO EN
U.S.A.

Printed in the U.S.A.

TO SOPHIA

Tales Contented

The Spring Tune

One calm and cloudless evening, towards the end of
April, Snufkin found himself far enough to the north
to see still unmelted patches of snow on the northern
slopes.

He had been walking all day through undisturbed landscapes, listening to the cries of the birds
also on their way northwards, home from the
South.

Walking had been easy, because his knapsack
was nearly empty and he had no worries on his
mind. He felt happy about the wood and the
weather, and himself. Tomorrow and yesterday were
both at a distance, and just at present the sun was

shining brightly red between the birches, and the air was cool and soft.

It's the right evening for a tune, Snufkin thought. A new tune, one part expectation, two parts spring sadness, and for the rest, just the great delight of walking alone and liking it.

He had kept this tune under his hat for several days, but hadn't quite dared to take it out yet. It had to grow into a kind of happy conviction. Then, he would simply have to put his lips to the mouth-organ, and all the notes would jump instantly in to their places.

If he released them too soon they might get stuck crossways and make only a half-good tune, or he might lose them altogether and never be in the right mood to get hold of them again. Tunes are serious things, especially if they have to be jolly and sad at the same time.

But this evening Snufkin felt rather sure of his tune. It was there, waiting, nearly full-grown—and it was going to be the best he ever made.

Then, when he arrived in Moominvalley he'd sit on the bridge rail and play it, and Moomintroll would say at once: That's a good one. Really a good one.

Snufkin stopped in his tracks, feeling just a little bit uneasy. Yes, Moomintroll, always waiting and longing. Moomintroll who sat at home, who waited for him and admired him, and who always told him: Of course you have to feel free. Naturally you must go away. I do understand that you have to be alone at times.

And all the times his eyes were black with disappointment and no one could help it.

Oh my, oh my, Snufkin said to himself and continued on his way.

Oh my, oh my. He's got such a lot of feelings, this Moomintroll. I won't think of him now. He's a splendid Moomin, but I don't have to think of him now. Tonight I'm alone with my tune, and tonight isn't tomorrow.

In a little while Snufkin had managed to forget all about Moomintroll. He was sniffing around for a good place to camp in, and when he heard a brook a bit further on in the wood he went towards the sound.

The last red ray of sunlight had vanished between the birches. Now came the spring twilight, slow and blue. All the wood was changed, and the white pillars of the birches went wandering further and further off in the blue dusk.

The brook was a good one.

It went rushing clear and brown over wads of last year's leaves, through small tunnels of left-over ice, swerving through the green moss and throwing itself headlong down in a small waterfall on to a white sand bottom. In places it droned sharp as a mosquito, then it tried to sound great and menacing, stopped, gurgled with a mouthful of melted snow, and laughed at it all.

Snufkin stood listening in the damp moss. I must have the brook in my tune also, he thought. In the refrain, I think.

A small stone suddenly came loose near the

waterfall and raised the pitch of the brook a whole octave.

Not bad, Snufkin said admiringly. That's the way to do it. A sudden change, just in passing. I'll have to find that brook a tune of its own.

He took out his old saucepan and filled it from the waterfall. Then he went in under the firs to look for firewood. The ground was still wet from the spring thaw and the rains, and Snufkin had to crawl far under a brambly windfall to find any dry sticks. When he reached out someone gave a sudden shout and flashed past him and off among the firs, still crying and squeaking all the way.

Oh yes, Snufkin said. Creeps and woodies everywhere. Funny how nervous they always seem to be. The smaller the jumpier.

He found a dried stump and some sticks and built himself a good camp-fire by the brook. Snufkin was used to cooking his own dinner. He never cooked a dinner for other people if he could avoid it, nor did he care much for other people's dinners. So many people insisted on talking when they had a meal.

Also they had a great liking for chairs and tables, and some of them used napkins. He even had heard of a hemulen who changed his clothes every time he was about to eat, but that was probably slander.

A little distractedly Snufkin ate his meagre soup while he rested his eyes on the green moss by the birches.

The tune was quite near at hand, easy to catch by the tail. But there was time enough to wait, it was hedged in and couldn't get away. No, better to wash the dishes first, then light a pipe—and afterwards, when the camp-fire was burning down and the night creatures started calling for each other, then he'd have it.

Snufkin was washing his saucepan in the brook when he caught sight of the creep. It was sitting on the far side below a tree root, looking at him. Its eyes were scared but very interested, following Snufkin's every movement.

Two shy eyes under a mop of hair. Just the look people have who are never noticed.

Snufkin pretended that he hadn't seen the creep. He raked up his fire and cut himself some fir twigs to sit on. He took out his pipe and lit it. He puffed a few clouds of smoke towards the night sky and waited for the spring tune.

It didn't come. Instead he felt the creep's eyes upon him. They watched everything he did,

admiringly, and he began to feel uneasy once more. He clapped his paws together and shouted: "Shoo! Be off!"

At this the creep slunk out from under the tree root—it was still on the other side of the brook— and said, very shyly: "I hope I haven't scared you? I know who you are. You're Snufkin."

And then the creep stepped straight into the water and started to wade across. The brook was rather too broad for it, and the water was ice-cold. A couple of times the creep lost its foothold and tumbled over, but Snufkin was feeling so uneasy that he simply didn't think of giving it a hand.

Finally a rather thin and miserable creep crawled ashore and said with chattering teeth: "Hello, I'm so happy to meet you."

"Hullo," Snufkin answered equally coldly.

"May I warm myself by your fire?" the creep continued, its wet little face shining with happiness. "Just think of it, then I'll be the creep who has sat by Snufkin's camp fire. I'll never forget that."

The creep edged closer, laid one paw on Snufkin's knapsack and solemnly whispered:

"Is this where you keep the mouth organ? Do you have it here?"

"Yes," Snufkin said, rather crossly. His tune was lost, loneliness was gone, all was different. He clenched his teeth around the pipe-stem and stared in among the birches without really seeing them.

"Now, don't mind me," the creep said innocently. "In case you'd like to play, I mean. You'd never

guess how I long for a little music. I've never heard
any. But I've heard about you. The hedgehog, and
Toffle, and my mother, they've all told me . . .
Toffle has even seen you, once! Yes, you can't
imagine . . . nothing much ever happens here . . .
But we dream lots and lots . . ."

"Well, what's your name," Snufkin asked. The
evening was spoiled anyway, so he thought it
easier to talk.

"I'm so small that I haven't got a name," the
creep said eagerly. "As a matter of fact, nobody's
even asked me about it before. And then I meet you,
whom I've heard so much about and always
longed to see, and the first thing you ask me is what
my name is! Do you think . . . perhaps you might . . .
I mean, would it be a lot of trouble for you to think
up a name for me, a name that would be only mine
and no one else could have it? Now, tonight?"

Snufkin mumbled something and pulled his hat
over his eyes. Someone flew across the brook on long
pointed wings and gave a long, sad cry among the
trees: Yo-yooo, yo-ooo, tee-woo . . .

"You can't ever be really free if you admire
somebody too much," Snufkin suddenly said, "I
know."

"I know you know everything," the little creep
prattled on, edging closer still. "I know you've seen
everything. You're right in everything you say, and
I'll always try to become as free as you are . . . So
now you're on your way to Moominvalley to have a
rest and meet your friends . . . The hedgehog told
me that Moomintroll started waiting for you as soon

as he wakes from winter sleep . . . Isn't it a nice thing to know that someone's longing for you and waiting and waiting to see you again?"

"I'm coming when it suits me," Snufkin cried violently. "Perhaps I shan't come at all. Perhaps I will go somewhere else."

"Oh. Then he'll be sad," said the creep.

Its fur was beginning to dry and becoming light brown and soft. It picked at the knapsack once again and asked cautiously:

"Would you perhaps . . . You who have travelled so much . . . ?"

"No," Snufkin said. And he thought angrily: Why can't they ever let my wanderings alone?! Can't they understand that I'll talk it all to pieces

if I have to tell about it. Then it's gone, and when I
try to remember what it really was like, I remember
only my own story.

There was a long silence, and the night bird
cried again.

The creep arose and said in a small voice:

"Well, I must be off, I think. Cheerio."

"Cheerio," Snufkin said, fidgeting a little, "Listen.
Er. That name you asked for. What about Teety-
woo, for instance. Teety-woo, don't you see, a light
beginning, sort of, and a little sadness to round it
off."

The little creep stared at him with yellow eyes in
the firelight. It thought its name over, tasted it,
listened to it, crawled inside it, and finally turned
its snout to the sky and softly howled its new name,
so sadly and ecstatically that Snufkin felt a shiver
along his back.

Then a brown tail disappeared in the brambles,
and all was silent.

"Golly," Snufkin said and kicked at an ember.
He rapped out his pipe. Then he rose and shouted:
"Hullo. Come back."

But the wood was silent. Oh, well, Snufkin
thought. You can't always be friendly. It's impossible, there isn't the time. And at least this creep
has got a name.

He sat down again and listened to the brook and
the silence, and waited for his tune to come back.
But it didn't come. He knew at once that it had
moved too far away to be caught. Perhaps he'd
never catch it. The only thing he seemed to hear

was the eager and shy voice of the creep, talking and talking and talking.

Why don't they keep at home with their mothers, Snufkin said crossly and threw himself on his back on to the fir twigs. After a while he sat up and shouted once more. He listened for a long time, then he pulled his hat over his snout and went to sleep.

*   *   *

The next morning Snufkin continued his march. He was tired and cross and trudged northwards without looking right or left. And not even the faintest beginning of a tune moved under his hat.

He simply could not think of anything but the creep. He remembered every single word it had said and every word he had said himself, and he chewed them over and over until he felt sick and had to sit down and rest.

What's come over me, Snufkin thought, angry and bewildered. I've never felt like this before. I must be ill.

He rose and continued his way, and it started all over again, everything the creep had told him and all he had said in reply.

Finally he had to stop. In the afternoon he turned about and started back.

After a while he felt better. He went faster and faster, he bubbled as he ran. Little tunes flitted about his ears but he hadn't the time to catch them. Towards evening he was back in the birch wood and started to call.

"Teety-woo!" he cried. "Teety-woo!" And the night birds awoke and answered him, tee-woo, tee-woo, but he heard nothing from the creep.

Snufkin walked back and forth, looking and calling and listening, until dusk had fallen. The new moon rose in a clearing, and Snufkin stood looking at it and feeling quite at a loss.

I ought to make a wish, he thought. It's a new moon.

He was about to wish for the usual thing: a new tune, or, as he sometimes did: a new road. But now he hastily corrected himself and said aloud: "To find Teety-woo."

Then he turned around three times and crossed the clearing, went into the wood and up a hill. Something rustled in the bushes, something light brown and furry.

"Teety-woo!" Snufkin called softly. "I've come back for a chat."

"Oh. Hello," Teety-woo replied and stuck out his head from the bushes, "That's splendid, because I've got something to show you. Look! A name plate! With my own name on it, to hang on my door when I get a house of my own." -

The creep showed him a piece of bark with an owner's mark on it, and continued importantly:

"Neat, isn't it? Everybody thinks so."

"Very!" Snufkin said. "So you'll have a house of your own?"

"Indeed!" the creep said excitedly, "I've moved away from home and begun living! It's so exciting! You see, before I had a name I just used to hop around, and perhaps feel this or that about this or that, and everything was simply happening around me, sometimes nice things and sometimes not nice, but nothing was real, don't you see?"

Snufkin started to reply, but the creep continued:

"Now I'm a person, and everything that happens *means* something. Because it doesn't only happen, it happens to *me*, Teety-woo. And Teety-woo may think this or think that about it, as the case may be —if you see what I mean?"

"Certainly, I see," said Snufkin. "That's good for you."

Teety-woo nodded and started to rummage in the bushes.

"Know what," Snufkin said, "I'm on my way to Moomintroll still. As a matter of fact I really want to see him."

"Oh?" said Teety-woo, "Moomintroll? Yes."

"Perhaps you'd like to hear some tunes before I have to start," Snufkin continued, "Or maybe a few stories?"

The creep stuck out its head and said:

"Stories? Oh, yes. Later tonight, perhaps. Just at the moment I'm in quite a hurry—I'm sure you don't mind . . ."

The light brown tail vanished in the heather, and after a while Teety-woo's ears came to view a bit further away, and he called out:

"Cheerio, and give my greetings to Moomintroll! I'll have to live as fast as I can, because I've lost a lot of time already!"

Then he was gone.

Snufkin scratched his head.

So, he said to himself. Yes. I see.

He stretched out on his back and looked up into the spring sky. It was a clear dark blue straight above him and sea green over the tree tops. Somewhere under his hat the tune began to move, one part expectation, and two parts spring sadness, and for the rest just a colossal delight at being alone.

A Tale of Horror

The next-to-youngest whomper was crawling along beside the back garden fence. Every now and then he lay quite still, watching the enemy, before he continued. His baby brother came crawling behind him.

By the vegetable patch the whomper flattened himself against the ground and sidled to cover among the lettuces. That was his only chance. The place was teeming with enemy scouts, and some of them swarmed in the air.

"I'm black all over," said his baby brother.

"Shut up, if you value your life," the whomper whispered back. "What colour do you expect to become in a mangrove swamp? Blue?"

"This is lettuce," said his baby brother.

"And you're going to be a grown-up in no time if you keep that up," the whomper said. "You'll be like daddy and mummy, and serve you right. Then you'll see and hear just ordinary things, I mean you'll see and hear simply nothing, and that's the end."

"Mphm," said his baby brother and started to eat a little earth.

"That's poisoned," the whomper said curtly. "And all the fruit in this country is poisoned too. And look, now they've spotted us, thanks to you."

Two scouts came humming down towards them across the pea rows, but the whomper killed them swiftly. Panting from excitement and exertion he slid down in the ditch and sat there, still as a frog. He listened so hard that it made his ears wobble and his head nearly burst. The rest of the scouts were keeping very quiet, but they were advancing all the time, creeping silently towards him through the grass. The prairie grass. They were innumerable.

"Listen," said his baby brother from the edge of the ditch. "I want to go home."

"You'll never see home again," his brother said glumly. "Your bones will lie bleaching on the prairie, and daddy and mummy'll weep till they drown, and there'll be nothing more left of you then, nothing at all, or just a little for the hyenas to howl over."

The whomper's baby brother opened his mouth, took a large breath and started to cry.

The whomper judged from the sound of it that this cry was going to last long. So he left his baby brother alone and crawled further along the ditch. He had lost every idea of the enemy's whereabouts, he didn't even know what the enemy looked like any more.

He felt tricked and thought: I wish baby brothers didn't exist. They should be born big or not at all. They don't know a thing about war. They should be kept in boxes until they understand.

The ditch was wet, and the whomper got up and began to wade along it. It was a large and very long ditch. He decided to discover the South Pole and continued his way, more and more exhausted each day, because his food and water were finished, and, for worse luck, a polar bear had bitten him in the leg.

Finally the ditch came to an end, disappearing in the earth, and the whomper was all alone at the South Pole.

He was standing on the marsh.

The marsh was grey and dark green, dotted with black gleaming pools. Lots of white cottongrass grew everywhere, like snow, and the air had a nice, musty smell.

The marsh is out of bounds, the whomper thought aloud. It's out of bounds to smaller whompers, and grown-up ones don't ever go there. But I'm the only

one who knows why it's dangerous. This is the place where the Ghost Wagon rolls by on its great and heavy wheels. You can hear its rumble from afar but no one's ever seen the driver . . .

Oh no! the whomper interrupted himself. Suddenly he felt cold and afraid, from his stomach upwards. A moment ago the Ghost Wagon hadn't existed. Nobody had ever heard of it. Then he thought it up, and there it was. Somewhere far away, waiting for the darkness to start rolling along.

I think, said the whomper, I rather think I'm a whomper who has looked and searched for his home for ten years. And now this whomper gets a sudden feeling that his home is somewhere quite near.

He sniffed for the right direction and set off. While he walked he thought a bit about mud snakes and live fungi that came crawling after one—until they were there and started to grow in the moss.

Those things could swallow up a baby brother in a jiffy, he thought sadly. Perhaps they've even done it already. They're everywhere. I fear the worst. But there is hope still, a relief expedition might save him.

He started to run.

Poor baby brother, the whomper thought. So small, and so silly. If the mud snakes have got him I'll have no baby brother any more, and then I'll be the youngest.

He sobbed and ran, his hair was damp from fright, he came darting over the yard, past the wood-shed, up the front steps, calling at the top of his voice:

"Mummy! Daddy! Baby brother's been eaten up!"

The whomper's mother was big and worried. She was always worried. Now she jumped to her feet and spilled peas from her pinafore all over the floor and cried:

"What? What! What are you saying? Where's baby brother? Haven't you looked after him?"

"Oh," said the whomper a little calmer, "he fell in a mud hole in the marsh. And almost at once a mud snake came out and wound itself around his fat little stomach and bit his nose off. Yes. I'm quite beside myself, but then what can one do? There's so many more mud snakes than baby brothers."

"Snake?" cried his mother.

But his father said: "Take it easy. He's telling fibs again. Mark my words." And the whomper's father quickly looked out of the window so as not to be worried, and saw that baby brother was sitting in the yard, busy eating sand.

"How many times have I told you not to tell stories," the whomper's daddy said, and his mummy cried a little and asked: "Should he have a smacking?"

"Probably," the whomper's daddy said, "but I don't feel up to it at the moment. If he'll just admit that lying is nasty."

"I've never lied," said the whomper.

"You told us that your baby brother was swallowed up, and he isn't swallowed up," his father explained.

"That's splendid, isn't it?" said the whomper.
"Aren't you happy? *I'm* terribly glad and relieved.
Those mud snakes can swallow anybody up in a
jiffy, you know. There's not even a bit left over,

nothing but desolation and night and the distant
laugh of the hyenas."

"Please," said his mother. "*Please.*"

"So all's well that ends well," the whomper
concluded happily. "Do we have dessert tonight?"

At this the whomper's daddy suddenly became
enraged and said: "Not for you, my boy. You'll get
no dinner at all until you understand that one
mustn't lie."

"Of course one mustn't," said the whomper
surprisedly. "It's a bad thing to do."

"You see how it is," said his mummy. "Now let
him have his dinner, he doesn't understand this at
all."

"No," said his daddy. "If I've said no dinner,
then it is no dinner."

Because this poor daddy had got the idea that the
whomper would never trust him any more if he
took a word back.

*   *   *

So the whomper had to go to bed at sundown,
and he felt very embittered towards his daddy and
mummy. Naturally they had behaved badly many
times before, but had never been quite as silly as
this. The whomper decided to go away. Not to
punish them, only because he suddenly felt so
utterly tired of them and their inability to understand what was important or dangerous.

They simply drew a line straight through all
things and declared that on one side of it everything

was believable and useful, and on the other side everything was simply thought up and useless.

I'd like to see them eye to eye with an Aitchumb, the whomper mumbled to himself when he padded downstairs and slunk out in the garden. Believe me, they'd be amazed! Or a mud snake, indeed. I could send them one in a box some day. With a glass lid, because I wouldn't want them swallowed up, not really.

The whomper went back to the forbidden marsh, because he had to show to himself that he was independent. The marsh had turned blue, nearly black, and the sky was green. There was a bright yellow streak of sundown by the horizon, that made the marsh look terribly large and gloomy.

Of course I'm not lying, said the whomper and went plodding along. It's all real. The enemy and the Aitchumb and the mud snakes and the Ghost Wagon. They're quite as real as our neighbours and the gardener and the hens and my scooter.

And then the whomper stood quite still in his tracks and listened.

Somewhere in the distance the Ghost Wagon started rolling, it whisked red sparks over the heather, it creaked and cracked and gathered speed.

You shouldn't have taken any notice of it from the first, the whomper told himself. Now it's coming. Run!

The grass tufts gave and slithered under his paws, black water holes looked at him like large eyes out of the sedge, and he could feel the mud squashing between his toes.

You mustn't think about the mud snakes, the whomper said, and so he thought of them, strong and clear, and they came creeping out of their holes at once, licking their moustaches.

I wish I were like my fat baby brother, the whomper cried in desperation. He thinks only with his tummy and stuffs himself with sand and earth. He even tried to eat his balloon once. We'd have lost him if he'd succeeded.

This thought enchanted the whomper and made him stop his running. A fat baby brother rising straight up in the air. His legs would be sticking helplessly out and the string dangling from his mouth . . .

Oh, no!

Far out on the marsh a light shone. It wasn't the Ghost Wagon, it was just a small square window with a steady light burning.

Now go there, the whomper told himself. Just walk, don't run, because running makes you scared. And don't think, just walk along.

      *   *   *

It was a circular house, so it probably belonged to some mymble or other. The whomper knocked at the door. He knocked several times, and as no one came to answer he opened it and went inside.

Inside was warm and nice. A lamp stood on the window-sill and made the night coal-black. A clock was ticking away somewhere, and atop a large wardrobe a very small mymble was lying on her stomach, looking down at him.

"Hello," said the whomper. "I've saved myself at the last minute. From mud snakes and live fungi! You've no idea!"

The small mymble regarded him silently and critically. Then she said:

"I'm My. I've seen you before. You were tending a fat little whomper and mumbling to yourself all the time and waving your paws about. Ha ha."

"Never you mind," said the whomper. "Why are you sitting on that wardrobe? That's silly."

"To some people," drawled little My. "To some people it may look silly. For me it's my only hope of escape from a horrible fate."

She leaned down over the edge of the wardrobe and whispered:

"The live fungi are already in the parlour."

"Eh," said the whomper.

"From up here I can see that they're sitting just behind the door," little My continued. "They're waiting. You'd better make that doormat into a roll and push it against the crack. Otherwise they'll flatten out and start to crawl in here under the door."

"But that can't be true," said the whomper,

feeling a lump in his throat. "Those fungi didn't even exist this morning. I've invented them."

"You did, did you?" little My said haughtily. "The sticky kind? The kind that grows into a sort of thick blanket and fastens itself on people?"

"I don't know," whispered the whomper. He trembled a little. "I don't know . . ."

"My granny is quite grown over with them," little My said. "She's in the parlour. Or what's left of her. She's just a large green lump, only her whiskers keep sprouting out at one end. You'd better push the carpet against that other door. It might help, but I'm not sure."

The whomper's heart was thumping hard and his paws felt so stiff that he had a hard job in rolling up the carpets. Somewhere in the house the clock went on slowly ticking.

"That's the sound the fungi make when they grow," little My explained. "They grow and grow until they burst the doors, and then they're free to crawl over you."

"Let me up on the wardrobe!" the whomper cried.

"Sorry, no room here," said little My.

There was a knock on the outer door.

"That's funny," said little My and sighed, "funny that they care to knock on doors when they can come in as they please . . ."

The whomper rushed to the wardrobe and tried to climb it. The knock was repeated.

"My! Someone's at the door!" a voice called from an inner room.

"I hear, I hear, I hear," little My called back.
"That was Granny," she explained to the whomper.
"It's strange that she's still able to speak."

The whomper stared at the parlour door. It

opened slowly, a black little crack. He gave a cry and rolled in under the sofa.

"My," Granny said, "haven't I told you to go and answer the door? And why have you rolled up the carpet? And why don't people ever let me sleep?"

She was a terribly old and cross Granny in a large white nightgown. She went to the outer door and opened it and said: "Good evening."

"Good evening," said the whomper's daddy. "I'm terribly sorry to disturb you at this hour. But I wonder if you've seen my boy, the next-to-youngest one . . ."

"He's under the sofa," little My said.

"You can come out," said the whomper's daddy. "No one's angry."

"Oh, under the sofa. Well," Granny said, a little tiredly. "Of course it's nice to have one's grand-children visiting, and naturally little My can always ask her little playmates to come here! But I wish they'd play in the daytime and not at nights."

"I'm so sorry," the daddy said quickly. "He'll come in the morning next time."

The whomper crawled out from under the sofa. He didn't look at My, nor at her Granny either. He walked straight for the door and out on the steps and into the dark.

His daddy walked beside him, saying nothing. The whomper felt so hurt that he was very near to tears.

"Daddy," he said. "That girl . . . you'd never believe . . . I'm not going back there, not in a thousand years," the whomper continued savagely. "She tricked me! She told such stories! She makes people sick with her lies!"

"I understand," said his daddy comfortingly. "Such things can be very unpleasant."

And they went home and ate all the dessert that was left over.

The Fillyjonk who believed in Disasters

Once upon a time there was a fillyjonk who was washing her large carpet in the sea. She rubbed it with soap and a brush up to the first blue stripe, and then she waited for a seventh wave to come and wash the soap away.

Then she soaped and rubbed further, to the next blue stripe, and the sun was warming her back, and she stood with her thin legs in the clear water, rubbing and rubbing.

It was a mild and motionless summer day, exactly right for washing carpets. Slow and sleepy swells came rolling in to help her with the rinsing, and around her red cap a few bumble-bees were humming: they took her for a flower!

Don't you pretend, the fillyjonk thought grimly.

I know how things are. Everything's always peaceful like this just before a disaster.

She reached the last blue stripe, let the seventh wave rinse it for a moment, and then pulled the whole of the carpet out of the water.

The smooth rock shone redly under the rippling water, reflections of light danced over the fillyjonk's toes and gilded all ten of them.

She stood and mused. A new cap, orange-red perhaps? Or one could embroider reflections of light around the edge of the old one? In gold? But of course it wouldn't look the same because they wouldn't move. And besides, what does one need a new cap for when danger breaks loose? One might just as well perish in the old one . . .

The fillyjonk pulled her carpet ashore and slapped it down on the rock and sullenly stalked over it to stamp the water from it.

The weather was far too fine, quite unnatural.

Something or other had to happen. She knew it.
Somewhere below the horizon something black and
terrible was lurking—working larger, drawing
nearer—faster and faster . . .

One doesn't even know what it is, the fillyjonk
whispered to herself.

Her heart began to thump and her back felt
cold, and she whirled around as if she had an enemy
behind her. But the sea was glittering as before,
the reflections danced over the floor in playful
twists, and the faint summer wind comfortingly
stroked her snout.

But it is far from easy to comfort a fillyjonk who
is stricken with panic and doesn't know why. With
shaking paws she spread her carpet to dry, scram-
bled together her soap and brush and went rushing
homewards to put the tea-kettle on the fire. Gaffsie
had promised to drop in at five o'clock.

*   *   *

The fillyjonk lived in a large and not very pretty
house. Someone, who had wanted to get rid of old
paint, had painted it dark green on the outside
and brown all over the inside. The fillyjonk had
rented it unfurnished from a hemulen who had
assured her that her grandmother used to live there
in the summer, when she was a young girl. And as
the fillyjonk was very attached to her kindred and
relatives she at once decided that she would honour
her grandmother's memory by living in the same
house.

The first evening she had sat on her doorstep and wondered about her grandmother who must have been very unlike herself in her youth. How curious that a genuine fillyjonk with a true sense of nature's beauty should have wanted to live on this glum and sandy shore! No garden to grow jam plums in! Not the smallest leafy tree or even bush to start an arbour with. Not even a nice view!

The fillyjonk sighed and looked forlornly at the green evening sea trimming the long beach with its breakers. Green water, white sand, red dried seaweed. An exact setting for disaster; not a single safe spot.

And afterwards, of course, the fillyjonk had found out that it was all a mistake. She had moved into this horrible house on this horrible beach quite unnecessarily. Her grandmother had lived elsewhere. That is life!

But by that time the fillyjonk had written letters to all her relatives about her summer house, and so she didn't think it proper to change her plans.

They might have thought her a little silly.

So the fillyjonk closed her door and tried to make the house cosy inside. This was not easy. The ceilings were so high that they always seemed full of shadows. The windows were large and solemn, and no lace curtains could give them a friendly look. They weren't windows for looking out of, they were windows to look in from—and the fillyjonk did not like this thought.

She tried to arrange cosy corners, but they never became cosy. Her furniture had a lost look. The chairs nestled close to the table, the sofa huddled against the wall, and the lighted patches around the lamps were as dejected as a flash-light in a dark wood.

Like all fillyjonks she owned a lot of knick-knacks. Small mirrors, photographs framed in red velvet and little shells, china kittens and hemulens resting on pieces of crochet work, beautiful maxims embroidered in silk or silver, very small vases and nice mymble-shaped tea-cosies—well, all sorts of things that make life more easy and less dangerous, and large.

But all these beloved things of beauty lost their

safety and their meaning in the bleak house by the sea. She moved them from table to sideboard and from sideboard to window-sill, but nowhere did they look right.

*   *   *

There they were again. Just as forlorn.

The fillyjonk stopped at the door and looked at her belongings to comfort herself. But they were just as helpless as she was. She went into the kitchen and laid the soap and scrubbing brush on the sink. Then she lighted the fire under the tea-kettle and took out her best gold-edged cups. She lifted down the cake-dish, nimbly blew off some crumbs and laid some iced little cakes on top of the others to impress Gaffsie.

Gaffsie never took milk with her tea, but the fillyjonk nevertheless put grandmother's little silver boat on the tray. The sugar lumps she shook out in a tiny plush basket with pearl-crusted handles.

While she set the tea-tray she felt quite calm and was able to shut off all thoughts of disaster.

It was a real pity that no nice flowers were to be found in this unlucky place. All the plants by the shore were cross and prickly little shrubs, and their flowers didn't match her drawing-room. The fillyjonk gave her table vase a displeased nudge and took a step towards the window to look for Gaffsie.

Then she thought hastily: No, no. I won't look for her. I'll wait for her knock. Then I run and answer the door, and we'll both be terribly delighted and sociable and have a good chat . . . If I look for her perhaps the beach will be quite empty all the way to the light-house. Or else I'll see just a tiny little spot coming, and I don't like to watch things that draw nearer and nearer . . . and still worse would it be, wouldn't it, if the little spot started to grow smaller and was going the other way . . .

The fillyjonk started to tremble. What's come over me, she thought. I mustn't talk about this with Gaffsie. She's really not the person I'd prefer to chat with at all, but then I don't know anybody else hereabouts.

There was a knock on the door. The fillyjonk went rushing out into the hall and was already talking on her way to the door.

". . . and what splendid weather," she shouted, "and the sea, did you look at the sea . . . how blue today, how friendly it looks, not a ripple! How are you, well, you look really radiant, and so I thought you would . . . But it's all this, of course, living like this, I mean, in the bosom of nature, and everything —it puts everything in order, doesn't it?"

She's more confused than usual, Gaffsie was thinking while she pulled off her gloves (because she was a real lady), and aloud she said:

"Exactly. How right you are, Mrs. Fillyjonk."

They sat down to the table, and the fillyjonk was so happy to have company that she prattled the sheerest nonsense and spilled tea all over the cloth.

Gaffsie said something nice about the cakes and the sugar bowl and everything she could think of,

but about the flower vase she said nothing, of
course. Gaffsie was a well-brought up person, and
anybody could see that that wild, angry shrub
didn't go well with the tea things.

After a while the fillyjonk stopped talking
nonsense, and as Gaffsie didn't say anything at all,
silence fell.

Then the sun clouded over and the table-cloth
suddenly looked grey. The large solemn windows
showed a mass of grey clouds, and the ladies could
hear a new kind of wind coming in from the sea.
Faint and far away, no more than a whisper.

"I saw you've had your carpet out for a wash,
Mrs. Fillyjonk," Gaffsie said with great civility.

"Yes, sea-water's said to be the right thing for
carpets," the fillyjonk replied. "The colours never
run, and there's such a lovely smell . . ."

I must make Gaffsie understand, she thought. I
have to tell somebody that I'm frightened, someone
who can answer me: But of course, I quite understand you must be. Or: Really, what on earth is
there to be afraid of? A splendid summer day like
today. Anything, but something.

"The cakes are my grandma's recipe," said the
fillyjonk. And then she leaned forward over the
table and whispered:

"This calm is unnatural. It means something
terrible is going to happen. Dear Gaffsie, believe
me, we are so very small and insignificant, and so
are our tea cakes and carpets and all those things,
you know, and still they're so important, but always
they're threatened by mercilessness . . ."

"Oh," said Gaffsie, feeling ill at ease.

"Yes, by mercilessness," the fillyjonk continued rather breathlessly. "By something one can't ask anything of, nor argue with, nor understand, and that never tells one anything. Something that one can see drawing near, through a black window-pane, far away on the road, far away to sea, growing and growing but not really showing itself until too late. Mrs. Gaffsie, have you felt it? Tell me that you know what I'm talking about! Please!"

Gaffsie was very red in the face and sat twirling the sugar bowl in her paws and wishing that she had never come.

"There can be very sudden storms at this time of the year," she said at last, cautiously.

The fillyjonk fell silent from disappointment. Gaffsie waited a while, then continued, slightly vexed:

"I hung out my washing last Friday, and believe me, there was such a wind quite suddenly that I found my best pillow-slips by the gate. What washing-material do you use, Mrs. Fillyjonk?"

"I don't remember," the fillyjonk answered, suddenly feeling very tired because Gaffsie didn't even try to understand her. "Would you like some more tea?"

"Thank you, not any more," Gaffsie said. "What a nice visit, only too short. I'm afraid I'll have to start on my way soon."

"Yes," the fillyjonk said, "I see."

Darkness was falling over the sea, and the beach was mumbling to itself. It was a bit too early to light the lamp, but still too dark to be nice. Gaffsie's narrow nose was more wrinkled than usually, and one could see that she didn't feel at ease. But the fillyjonk didn't help her to take her leave, she didn't say a word but sat quite still, only breaking a couple of iced cakes into crumbs.

How painful, Gaffsie thought and smuggled her handbag under her arm. The south-wester slightly raised its voice outside.

"You were talking about wind," the fillyjonk said suddenly. "A wind that carries off your washing. But I'm speaking about cyclones. Typhoons, Gaffsie dear. Tornadoes, whirlwinds, sand-storms . . . Flood waves that carry houses away . . . But most of all I'm talking about myself and my fears, even if I know that's not done. I know everything will turn out badly. I think about that all the time. Even while I'm washing my carpet. Do you understand that? Do you feel the same way?"

"Have you tried vinegar," said Gaffsie, staring into her teacup. "The colours keep best if you have a little vinegar in the rinsing water."

At this the fillyjonk became angry, which was a most unusual thing. She felt that she had to challenge Gaffsie in some way or other, and she chose the first thing that came to her mind. She pointed a shaking finger at the horrid little shrub in the table vase and cried:

"Look! Isn't it nice? The perfect thing to match my tea-set!"

And Gaffsie was feeling just as tired and cross, so she jumped to her feet and replied:

"Not a bit! It's all too large and prickly and

gaudy, it has a brazen look and doesn't belong on a tea-table at all!"

Then the two ladies took leave of each other, and the fillyjonk shut her door and went back to her drawing-room.

She felt miserable and disappointed with her tea party. The small shrub stood on the table, grey and thorny and covered with little dark red flowers. Suddenly it seemed to the fillyjonk that it wasn't the flowers that did not match her tea-set. It was the tea-set that didn't match anything.

She put the vase on the window-sill.

The sea had changed. It was grey all over, but the waves had bared their white teeth and were snapping at the beach. The sky had a ruddy glow, and looked heavy.

The fillyjonk stood in her window for a long time, listening to the rising wind.

Then there was a ring on the telephone.

"Is that Mrs. Fillyjonk?" Gaffsie's voice asked cautiously.

"Of course," said the fillyjonk. "No one else lives here. Did you arrive home all right?"

"Yes, all right," said Gaffsie. "There's quite a wind." She was silent for a while, and then she said in a friendly voice: "Mrs. Fillyjonk? Those terrible things you spoke of. Have they happened often to you?"

"No," said the fillyjonk.

"Just a few times, then?"

"Well, never, really," said the fillyjonk. "It's just how I feel."

"Oh," said Gaffsie. "Well, thank you for inviting

me. It was so nice. So nothing has ever happened to you?"

"No," said the fillyjonk. "So kind of you to call me. I hope we'll see more of each other."

"So do I," said Gaffsie and hung up.

The fillyjonk sat looking at the telephone for a while. She suddenly felt cold.

My windows are going dark again, she thought. I could hang some blankets against them. I could turn the mirrors face to wall. But she didn't do anything, she sat listening to the wind that had started to howl in the chimney. Not unlike a small homeless animal.

On the south side the hemulen's fishing net had started whacking against the wall, but the fillyjonk didn't dare go out to lift it down.

The house was shivering, very slightly. The wind was coming on in rushes; one could hear a gale getting an extra push on its way in from the sea.

A roof-tile went coasting down the roof and crashed to the ground. The fillyjonk rose and hurried into her bedroom. But it was too large, it didn't feel safe. The pantry. It would be small enough. The fillyjonk took her quilt from the bed and ran down the kitchen passage, kicked open the pantry door and shut it behind her. She panted a bit. Here you heard less of the gale. And here was no window, only a small ventilator grating.

She felt her way in the dark past the sack of potatoes and rolled herself into her quilt, on the floor below the jam shelf.

Slowly her imagination started to picture a gale of its own, very much blacker and wilder than the one that was shaking her house. The breakers grew to great white dragons, a roaring tornado sucked up the sea like a black pillar on the horizon, a gleaming pillar that came rushing towards her, nearer and nearer . . .

Those storms of her own were the worst ones. And deep down in her heart the fillyjonk was just a little proud of her disasters that belonged to no one else.

Gaffsie is a jackass, she thought. A silly woman with cakes and pillow-slips all over her mind. And she doesn't know a thing about flowers. And least of all about me. Now she's sitting at home thinking that I haven't ever experienced anything. I, who see the end of the world every day, and still I'm going on putting on my clothes, and taking them off again, and eating and washing-up the dishes and receiving visits, just as if nothing ever happened!

The fillyjonk thrust out her nose from the quilt, stared severely out in the dark and said: "I'll show you."

Whatever that meant. Then she snuggled down under her quilt and pressed her paws against her ears.

*   *   *

But outside the gale was steadily rising towards midnight, and by one o'clock it had reached 47 yards

per second (or however they measure the big storms).

About two o'clock in the morning the chimney blew down. Half of it fell outside the house and the other half smashed down into the kitchen fireplace. Through the hole in the ceiling one could see the dark night sky and great rushing clouds. And then the gale found its way inside and nothing at all was to be seen except flying ashes, wildly fluttering curtains and tablecloths, and photographs of aunts and uncles whirling through the air. All the filly-jonk's sacred things came to life, rustling, tinkling and clashing everywhere, doors were banging and pictures crashing to the floor.

In the middle of the drawing-room stood the fillyjonk herself, dazed and wild in her fluttering skirt, thinking confusedly: this is it. Now comes the end. At last. Now I don't have to wait any more.

She lifted the telephone receiver to call Gaffsie and tell her . . . well, tell her a few really crushing things. Coolly and triumphantly.

But the telephone wires had blown down.

The fillyjonk could hear nothing but the gale and the rattle of loosening roof-tiles. If I were to go up to the attic the roof would blow off, she thought. And if I go down in the cellar the whole house comes down over me. It's going to do it anyway.

She got hold of a china kitten and pressed it hard in her paw. Then a window blew open and shattered its pane in small fragments over the floor. A gust of rain spattered the mahogany furniture, and the stately plaster hemulen threw himself from his pedestal and went to pieces.

With a sickening crash her great chandelier fell to the floor. It had belonged to her maternal uncle. All around her the fillyjonk heard her belongings cry and creak. Then she caught a flash of her own pale snout in a fragment of a mirror, and without any further thought she rushed up to the window and jumped out.

She found herself sitting in the sand. She felt warm raindrops on her face, and her dress was fluttering and flapping around her like a sail.

She shut her eyes very tight and knew that she was in the midst of danger, totally helpless.

The gale was blowing, steady and undisturbed. But all the alarming noises had vanished, all the howling and crashing, the thumping, splintering and tearing. The danger had been inside the house, not outside.

The fillyjonk drew a wary breath, smelt the bitter tang of the sea-weed, and opened her eyes.

The darkness was no longer as dark as it had been in her drawing-room.

She could see the breakers and the light-house's outstretched arm of light that slowly moved through the night, passing her, wandering off over the sand dunes, losing itself towards the horizon, and returning again. Round and round circled the calm light, keeping an eye on the gale.

I've never been out alone at night before, the fillyjonk thought. If mother knew . . .

She started to crawl against the wind, down to the beach, to get as far away as possible from the hemulen's house. She still held the china kitten in her left paw, it calmed her to have something to protect. Now she could see that the sea looked almost all blue-white. The wave crests were blown straight off and drifted like smoke over the beach. The smoke tasted of salt.

Behind her something or other was still crashing to pieces, inside the house. But the fillyjonk didn't even turn her head. She had curled up behind a large boulder and was looking wide-eyed into the dark. She wasn't cold any longer. And the strange thing was that she suddenly felt quite safe. It was a very strange feeling, and she found it indescribably nice. But what was there to worry over? The disaster had come at last.

*   *   *

Towards morning the gale was blowing itself out. The fillyjonk hardly noticed it. She was sitting in deep thought about herself and her disasters, and her furniture, and wondering how it all fitted together. As a matter of fact nothing of consequence had happened, except that the chimney had come down.

But she had a feeling that nothing more important had ever happened to her in her life. It had given her quite a shaking-up and turned everything topsy-tuvy. The fillyjonk didn't know what she should do to right herself again.

The old kind of fillyjonk was lost, and she wasn't sure that she wanted her back. And what about all the belongings of this old fillyjonk?

All the things that were broken and sooty and

cracked and wet? To sit and mend it all, week after week, glueing and patching and looking for lost pieces and fragments . . .

To wash and iron and paint over and to feel sorry about all the irreparable things, and to know that there would still be cracks everywhere, and that all the things had been in such better shape before . . . No, no! And to put them all back into place in the dark and bleak rooms and try to find them cosy once more. . . .

No, I won't! cried the fillyjonk and rose on cramped legs. If I try to make everything the same as before, then I'll be the same myself as before. I'll be afraid once more . . . I can feel that. And the tornadoes will come back to lurk around me, and the typhoons too . . .

For the first time she looked back at the hemulen's house. It was standing as before. It was filled with broken things. It waited for her to come and take care of them.

No genuine fillyjonk had ever left her old inherited belongings adrift . . . Mother would have reminded me about duty, the fillyjonk mumbled. It was morning.

The eastern horizon was waiting for sunrise. Small frightened squalls of rain were flying off, and the sky was strewn with clouds that the gale had forgotten to take along with it. A few weak thunderclaps went rolling by.

The weather was uneasy and didn't know its own mind. The fillyjonk hesitated also.

At this moment she caught sight of the tornado.

It didn't look like her own special tornado, which was a gleaming black pillar of water. This was the real thing. It was luminous. It was a whirl of white clouds churning downwards in a large spiral, and it turned to chalk white where it met the water lifting itself upwards out of the sea.

It didn't roar, it didn't rush. It was quite silent and slowly came nearer the shore, slightly swaying on its way. The sun rose, and the tornado turned rose-petal red.

It looked infinitely tall, rotating silently and powerfully around itself, and it drew slowly nearer and nearer . . .

The fillyjonk was unable to move. She was standing still, quite still, crushing the china kitten in her paw and thinking: Oh, my beautiful, wonderful disaster . . .

The tornado wandered over the beach, not far from the fillyjonk. The white, majestic pillar passed her, became a pillar of sand, and very quietly lifted the roof off the hemulen's house. The fillyjonk saw it rise in the air and disappear. She saw her furniture go whirling up and disappear. She saw all her knick-knacks fly straight to heaven, tray-cloths and photo-frames and tea-cosies and grandma's silver cream jug, and the sentences in silk and silver, every single thing! and she thought ecstatically: How very, very wonderful! What can I do, a poor little fillyjonk, against the great powers of nature? What is there to mend and repair now? Nothing! All is washed clean and swept away!

The tornado went solemnly wandering off over

the fields, and she saw it taper off, break and disperse. It wasn't needed any more.

The fillyjonk drew a deep breath. Now I'll never be afraid again, she said to herself. Now I'm free. Now I can do anything.

She placed the china kitten on a boulder. It had lost an ear during the night and got a blob of black oil on its nose. It had a new look, slightly impish and cheeky.

The sun rose higher. The fillyjonk went down to the wet sand. There lay her carpet. The sea had decorated it with seaweed and shells, and no carpet had ever been more thoroughly rinsed. The fillyjonk chuckled. She lifted the carpet in both paws and pulled it after her out in the swells.

She dived headlong in a large green swell, she sat on her carpet and surfed on sizzling white foam, she dived again, down and down.

One swell after the other came rolling over her, transparently green, and then the fillyjonk came to the surface again, for a breath, and to look at the sun, spluttering and laughing and shouting and dancing with her carpet in the surf.

Never in her life had she had such fun.

Gaffsie had been shouting and calling for several minutes before the fillyjonk caught sight of her.

"How terrible!" shouted Gaffsie. "Dear, poor little Mrs. Fillyjonk!"

"Good morning!" said the fillyjonk and pulled her carpet to the beach.

"How are you today?"

"I'm beside myself," Gaffsie cried. "What a

night! I've thought of you all the time. And I saw
it myself! I saw it coming! What a disaster!"

"How do you mean?" asked the fillyjonk innocently.

"How right you were, how very right," said
Gaffsie. "You *said* there was a disaster coming. Oh,
all your beautiful things! Your beautiful home! I've
tried to call you all night, I was so worried, but the
line had blown down . . ."

"That was kind of you," said the fillyjonk and
wrenched the water from her cap. "But really quite
unnecessary. If you feel worried there's nothing like
putting a little vinegar in the rinsing water. Then
the colours keep!"

And the fillyjonk sat down in the sand and wept
with laughter.

The Last Dragon in the World

One Thursday, one of the last of the dog-days, Moomintroll caught a small dragon in the brown pond to the right of Moominpappa's hammock-tree.

Of course he hadn't dreamed of catching a dragon. He had hunted for a few of those small wobbly things that were rowing about in the bottom mud, because he wanted to know how they moved their legs when swimming, and whether they always swam backwards. But when he lifted his glass jar against the light there was something altogether different in it.

"By my everlasting tail," Moomintroll whispered, overawed. He held the jar between both paws and could only stare.

The dragon was no bigger than a matchbox, and it swam around with graceful strokes of its transparent wings that were as beautiful as the fins of a goldfish.

But no goldfish was as splendidly golden as this miniature dragon. It was sparkling like gold; it was knobbly with gold in the sunlight, the small head was emerald green and its eyes were lemon yellow. The six golden legs had each a green little paw, and the tail turned green toward the tip. It was a truly wonderful dragon.

Moomintroll screwed the lid on the jar (there were breathing-holes) and carefully put it down in the moss. Then he stretched himself out beside the jar and took a closer look.

The dragon swam close to the glass wall and opened its small jaws. They were packed with tiny white teeth.

It's angry, Moomintroll thought. It's angry even if it's so very small. What can I do to make it like me? . . . And what does it eat? What do dragons feed on?

A little worried and anxious he lifted the jar in his arms and started homewards, cautiously, so as not to make the dragon hurt itself against the glass walls. It was so very small and delicate.

"I'll keep you and pet you and love you," Moomintroll whispered. "You can sleep on my pillow. When you grow up and start liking me I'll take you for swims in the sea . . ."

*   *   *

Moominpappa was working on his tobacco patch. One could always show him the dragon and ask him about it. Or still, perhaps better not. Not yet. One could keep it a secret for a few days, until it had become used to people. And until one had had the greatest fun of all: showing it to Snufkin.

Moomintroll pressed the jar hard against him and went strolling towards the back door as indifferently as possible. The others were somewhere on the front side by the verandah. At the moment when Moomintroll slunk up the back steps little My jumped in to view from behind the water barrel and called:

"What've you got?"

"Nothing," said Moomintroll.

"A jar," said My, craning her neck. "What's in it? Why are you hiding it?"

Moomintroll rushed upstairs and into his room. He put the jar on the table. The water was sloshing about, and the dragon had wound his wings around him and curled up into a ball. Now it slowly straightened out and showed its teeth.

It won't happen again, Moomintroll promised.
I'm so sorry, dearest. He screwed off the lid, so as
to give the dragon a better view, and then he went
to the door and put the latch on. You never knew
with My.

When he returned to the dragon it had crawled
out of the water and was sitting on the edge of the
jar. Moomintroll cautiously stuck out a paw to
fondle it.

At this the dragon opened its jaws again and blew
out a small cloud of smoke. A red tongue darted
out like a flame and vanished again...

"Ow," said Moomintroll, because he had burned
himself. Not much, but distinctly.

He admired the dragon more than ever.

"You're angry, aren't you?" he asked in a low
voice. "You're terribly wild and cruel and wicked,
are you, what? Oh you sweet little goody-goody-
goo!"

The dragon snorted.

Moomintroll crawled under his bed and pulled out his night box. In it were a couple of small pancakes, now a little dried, half a piece of bread and butter, and an apple. He cut small pieces from them all and laid the morsels on the table in a circle around the dragon. It sniffed at them, gave him a contemptuous look and suddenly ran surprisingly nimbly to the window, where it attacked a large August fly.

The fly stopped humming and started to screech. The dragon already had its small green forepaws around its neck and blew a little smoke in its eyes.

And then the small white teeth went snippity-snap, the jaws came open, and the August fly disappeared. The dragon swallowed twice, licked its snout, scratched its ear and gave Moomintroll a scoffing, one-eyed glance.

"How clever you are!" cried Moomintroll. "My little teeny-weeny-poo!"

Just then Moominmamma beat the lunch gong downstairs.

"Now wait for me and be good," Moomintroll said. "I'll be back soon."

He stood for a moment looking longingly at the dragon, that didn't appear to be cuddly in the least. Then he whispered: "Little dearie," and ran downstairs and out on the verandah.

Even before her spoon had touched her porridge My started off:

"Certain people seem to be hiding secrets in mysterious glass jars."

"Shut up," said Moomintroll.

"One is led to believe," My continued, "that certain people are keeping leeches or wood-lice or why not very large centipedes that multiply a hundred times a minute."

"Mother," Moomintroll said. "You know, I've always wished for some small pet that was attached to me, and if I would ever have one, then it should be, or would . . ."

"How much wood would a wood louse chuck," said My and blew bubbles in her milk glass.

"What?" asked Moominpappa and looked up from his newspaper.

"Moomintroll has found a new animal," Moominmamma explained. "Does it bite?"

"It's so small it can't bite very hard," her son mumbled.

"And when will it grow up?" asked the Mymble. "When can one have a look at it? Does it talk?"

Moomintroll was silent. Now all was spoiled again. One ought to have the right to have a secret and to spring it as a surprise. But if you live inside a family you have neither. They know about everything from the start, and nothing's any fun after that.

"I'm going down to the river after lunch," Moomintroll said, slowly and contemptuously. Contemptuously as a dragon. "Mother, please tell them that they're not to go into my room. I can't answer for the consequences."

"Good," said Moominmamma and gave My a look, "Not a living soul may open his door."

Moomintroll finished his porridge in dignified silence. Then he went out, through the garden down to the bridge.

*   *   *

Snufkin was sitting before his tent, painting a cork float. Moomintroll looked at him, and straight away he felt happy over his dragon again.

"Whew," he said. "Families are a cross sometimes."

Snufkin grunted in agreement without taking his pipe from his mouth. They sat silent for a while, in male and friendly solidarity.

"By the way," Moomintroll suddenly said. "Have you ever come across a dragon on your wanderings?"

"You don't mean salamanders, lizards or crocodiles, apparently," Snufkin replied after a long silence. "You mean a dragon. No. Never. They're extinct."

"But there *might* be one left," Moomintroll said slowly, "and some one might even catch it in a glass jar some day."

Snufkin gave him a sharp look and saw that Moomintroll was about to burst from delight and suspense. So he replied quite curtly:

"I don't believe it."

"Possibly it would be no bigger than a matchbox even if it could spit fire all right," Moomintroll continued with a yawn.

"Well, that's pure fantasy, of course," said Snufkin who knew how surprises are prepared.

His friend stared past him and said:

"A dragon of pure gold with tiny green paws, who'd be devoted to one and follow one everywhere . . ."

And then Moomintroll jumped to his feet and cried: "I've found it! I've found a real dragon of my own!"

*   *   *

While they walked up to the house Snufkin went through the whole scale of disbelief, astonishment and wonder. He was perfect.

They went upstairs, opened the door with great caution, and went in.

The jar of water stood on the table as before, but the dragon had disappeared from it. Moomintroll looked under the bed, behind the chest of drawers, and all over the floor, calling all the while:

"Little friend . . . my pretty-pretty . . . my teeny-weeny, where are you . . ."

"Moomin," Snufkin said, "it's sitting on the window curtain."

So it was, high on the rod near the ceiling.

"How on earth," cried Moomintroll in great alarm. "He mustn't fall down . . . Keep quite still. Wait a bit . . . don't talk . . ."

He pulled the bedclothes from his bed and spread them on the floor below the window. Then he took the hemulen's old butterfly net and reached up towards the dragon.

"Jump!" he whispered. "Teeny-weeny . . . don't be afraid, it can't hurt you . . ."

"You'll frighten it away," said Snufkin.

The dragon yawned and hissed. It gave the butterfly net a good bite and started to purr like a small engine. And suddenly it flapped out under the ceiling and began flying around in circles.

"He's flying, he's flying!" Moomintroll shouted "My dragon's flying!"

"Of course," said Snufkin. "Don't jump about so. Keep still."

The dragon was hanging quite still in the air. Its wings were a blur, like a moth's. And then suddenly dived down, bit Moomintroll in the ear, so he gave a cry, and then it flew straight to Snufkin and settled on his shoulder.

It edged closer against his ear, closed its eyes and started to purr.

"What a funny creature," Snufkin said in astonishment. "It's all hot and glowing. What does it do?"

"It's liking you," said Moomintroll.

*   *   *

In the afternoon the Snork Maiden came home from visiting little My's grandma and of course was told at once that Moomintroll had found a dragon.

It was sitting on the verandah table beside Snufkin's cup of coffee, licking its paws. It had bitten everybody except Snufkin, and every time it became cross at anything it burned a hole somewhere.

"What a sweetie-pie," said the Snork Maiden. "What's its name?"

"Nothing special," Moomintroll mumbled. "It's just a dragon."

He let his paw warily crawl across the table until it touched one of the little gilded legs. At once the dragon whirled around, hissed at him and blew a small cloud of smoke.

"How sweet!" the Snork Maiden cried.

The dragon ran over to Snufkin's pipe that was

lying at the table, and sniffed at the bowl. Where it had sat was a round brown-edged hole in the table cloth.

"I wonder if it can burn through oilcloth too," Moominmamma said.

"Naturally," said little My. "Just wait until it's grown a bit. It'll burn down the house for us."

She grabbed a piece of cake, and the dragon rushed at her like a small golden fury and bit her in the paw.

"You d . . . d spider!" cried My, and slapped at the dragon with her napkin.

"If you say things like that you'll never go to heaven," the Mymble started instantly, but Moomintroll cut her short with a cry:

"It wasn't the dragon's fault! He thought you wanted the fly that was sitting on the cake."

"You and your dragon!" cried My whose paw was really hurting badly. "It isn't yours even, it's Snufkin's, because it likes only him!"

There was a silence.

"Did I hear the small fry squeak," said Snufkin and rose from the table. "A few hours more and it'll know where it belongs. Well. Be off. Fly to master!"

But the dragon had settled on Snufkin's shoulder again and clung to it with all six clawed paws, purring all the while like a sewing machine. Snufkin picked it up between thumb and forefinger and put it under the tea-cosy. Then he opened the glass door and went out into the garden.

"Oh, he'll suffocate," Moomintroll said and lifted the tea-cosy half an inch off the table. The

dragon came out like lightning, flew straight to the window and sat there staring after Snufkin, with its paws against the pane. After a little while it began to whine, and its golden colour turned to grey from neck to tail.

"Dragons," Moominpappa broke the silence, "disappeared from public consciousness about seventy years ago. I've looked them up in the encyclopaedia. The last to keep alive was the emotional species with strong combustion. They are most stubborn and never change their mind about anything . . ."

"Thanks for the tea," Moomintroll said and rose from the table. "I'm going upstairs."

"Darling, shall we leave your dragon here on the verandah?" Moominmamma asked. "Or are you taking it along with you?"

Moomintroll didn't reply.

He went to the door and opened it. There was a flash as the dragon swished past him, and the Snork Maiden cried:

"Oh! You won't catch it again! Why did you? I hadn't even looked at it properly yet!"

"Go and look for Snufkin," Moomintroll said between clenched teeth. "It will be sitting on his shoulder."

"My darling," Moominmamma said sadly. "My little troll."

*   *   *

Snufkin had barely got his fishing line baited when the dragon came buzzing and settled on his knee. It nearly tied itself into knots from delight at having found him.

"Well, this is a pretty kettle," Snufkin said and whisked the creature away. "Shoo. Be off with you, Go home!"

But of course he knew it was no use. The dragon would never leave him. And for all he knew it could live a hundred years.

Snufkin looked a little sadly at the small shining creature that was doing all it could to attract his attention.

"Yes, you're nice," he said. "Yes, it would be fun to have you along. But, don't you see, there's Moomintroll . . ."

The dragon yawned. It flew to his ragged hat brim and curled up to sleep on it. Snufkin sighed and cast his line into the river. His new float bobbed in the current, shining brightly red. He knew that Moomintroll wouldn't like fishing today. The Groke take it all . . .

The hours went by.

The little dragon flew off and caught some flies and returned to sleep on the hat. Snufkin got five roaches and one eel that he let off again because it made such a fuss.

Towards evening a boat came down the river. A youngish hemulen steered.

"Any luck?" he asked.

"So so," Snufkin replied. "Going far?"

"Oh, well," said the hemulen.

"Throw me your painter," Snufkin said. "You might have use for a few fish. Swaddle them in damp newspapers and roast them on the embers. It's not too bad."

"And what do *you* want?" asked the hemulen who wasn't used to presents.

Snufkin laughed and took off his hat with the sleeping dragon.

"Now listen," he said. "Take this with you as far as you're going and leave it in some nice place where there are a lot of flies. Fold up the hat to look like a nest, and put it under a bush or something to make this dragon feel undisturbed."

"A dragon, is it?" the hemulen asked suspiciously. "Does he bite? How often does one have to feed him?"

Snufkin went into his tent and returned with his old teakettle. He shoved a tuft of grass down into it and cautiously let the sleeping dragon down after it. Then he placed the lid firmly on and said:

"You can poke some flies down the nozzle now and then, and pour in a few drops of water sometimes also. Don't mind if the kettle becomes hot. Here you are. After a couple of days you can leave it."

"That's quite a job for five roaches," the hemulen replied sourly and hauled home his painter. The boat started to glide with the current.

"Don't forget the hat," Snufkin called over the water. "It's very particular about my hat."

"No, no no," said the hemulen and disappeared round the bend.

"He'll burn his fingers some time," Snufkin thought. "Might serve him right."

*   *   *

Moomintroll came after sundown.

"Hello," Snufkin said.

"Yippee," Moomintroll said tonelessly. "Caught any fish?"

"So so," Snufkin replied. "Won't you sit down?"

"Oh, I just happened to pass by," Moomintroll mumbled.

There was a pause. A new kind of silence, troubled and awkward. Finally Moomintroll asked:

"Does he shine in the dark?"

"Who?"

"Oh, the dragon. I just thought it might be fun to ask if a creep like that shines in the dark."

"I really don't know," Snufkin said. "You'd better go home and take a look."

"But I've let him out," Moomintroll cried. "Didn't he come to you?"

"Nope," Snufkin said, lighting his pipe. "Dragons, they do as they like. They're pretty flighty you know, and if they see a fat fly somewhere they forget everything else. That's dragons. They're really nothing much."

Moomintroll was silent for quite a while. Then he sat down in the grass and said:

"Perhaps you're right. Perhaps it was just as well that it went away. Well, yes. I rather think so. Snufkin. That new float of yours. I suppose it looked good in the water. The red one."

"Not bad," Snufkin said. "I'll make you one. Were you planning to fish tomorrow?"

"Of course," Moomintroll said. "Naturally."

The Hemulen who loved Silence

Once upon a time there was a hemulen who worked in a pleasure-ground, which doesn't necessarily mean having a lot of fun. The hemulen's job was to punch holes in tickets, so that people wouldn't have fun more than once, and such a job is quite enough to make anyone sad if you have to do it all your life.

The hemulen punched and punched, and while punching he used to dream of the things he would do when he got his pension at last.

In case someone doesn't know what a pension is, it means that you can do what you like in all the peace you wish for, when you're old enough. At least that was how the hemulen's relatives had explained it to him.

He had terribly many relatives, a great lot of enormous, rollicking, talkative hemulens who went about slapping each others' backs and bursting into gigantic laughs.

They were joint owners of the pleasure-ground, and in their spare time they blew the trombone or threw the hammer, told funny stories and frightened people generally. But they did it all with the best of intentions.

The hemulen himself didn't own anything because he was on the side-line, which means only half a relative, and as he never could put his foot down about anything to anyone he always had to do the baby-sitting, to work the big bellows of the merry-go-round, and, most of the time, to punch tickets.

"You're lonely and have nothing to do," the other hemulens used to tell him in their friendly way. "So it might cheer you up a bit to lend a hand and be among people."

"But I'm never lonely," the hemulen tried to explain. "I can't find the time to be. There's always such a lot of people who want to cheer me up. If you don't mind, I'd like so much to . . ."

"Splendid," the relatives said and slapped his back. "That's the thing. Never lonely, always on the go."

The hemulen punched along, dreaming about a great wonderful silent loneliness and hoped he would grow old as soon as possible.

The whirligigs whirled, the trombones trumpeted, gaffsies and whompers and mymbles shrieked in the roller coaster every night. Edward the Booble won a first prize in china smashing, and all around the sad and dreamy hemulen people danced and whooped, laughed and quarrelled and ate and drank, and by and by the hemulen grew simply

afraid of noisy people who were enjoying themselves.

He used to sleep in the hemulen childrens' dormitory, that was bright and nice in the daytime, and at nights when the kiddies awoke and cried he comforted them with a barrel-organ.

The rest of his spare time he lent a hand anywhere it was needed in a large house full of hemulens, and so he had company around the clock, and everybody was in high spirits and told him all about everything they thought and did and planned to do. Only they never gave him time to reply properly.

"Won't I grow old soon?" the hemulen once asked at dinner.

"Old? You?" his uncle shouted. "Far from it. Buck up, buck up, nobody's older than he feels."

"But I feel really old," the hemulen said hopefully.

"Pish, posh," the uncle said. "We're going to have extra spot of fireworks tonight, and the brass band will play until sunrise."

But the fireworks never were touched off, because that same afternoon a great rain started to fall. It continued all night and all the next day, and the next one after that, and then all the following week.

To tell the truth this rain kept up for eight weeks without a stop. No one had ever seen the like.

The pleasure-ground lost its colours, shrunk and

withered away like a flower. It paled and rusted, and then it slowly started to disperse, because it was built on sand.

The roller coaster railway caved in with a sigh, and the merry-go-rounds went slowly turning around in large grey pools and puddles, until they were swept off, faintly tinkling, by the new rivers that were formed by the rain. All small kiddies, toffles and woodies and whompers and mymbles, and so forth, were standing days on end with their snouts pressed to the window-panes, looking at their July becoming drenched and their colour and music floating away.

The House of Mirrors came crashing down in millions of wet splinters, and pink drenched paper roses from the Miracle Garden went bobbing off in hundreds over the fields. Over it all rose the wailing chorus of the kiddies.

They were driving their parents to desperation, because they hadn't a single thing to do except grieve over the lost pleasure-ground.

Streamers and empty balloons were drooping from the trees, the Happy House was filled with mud, and the three-headed alligator swam off to the sea. He

left two of his heads behind him, because they had been glued on.

The hemulens took it all as a splendid joke. They stood at their windows, laughing and pointing and slapping backs, and shouted:

"Look! There goes the curtain to the Arabian Nights! The dancing floor has come loose! There's five black bats from the Cave of Horror on the fillyjonk's roof! Did you ever!"

They decided in the best of spirits to start a skating rink instead, when the water froze, of course —and they tried to comfort the hemulen by promising him the ticket punching job again as soon as they could get things going.

"No," the hemulen suddenly said. "No, no, no. I don't want to. I want my pension. I want to do what I feel like doing, and I want to be absolutely alone in some silent place."

"But my dear nephew," one of his uncles said with enormous astonishment, "Do you mean what you say?"

"I do," said the hemulen. "Every word of it."

"But why haven't you told us before?" the perplexed relatives asked him. "We've always believed that you've enjoyed yourself."

"I never dared tell you," the hemulen admitted.

At this they all laughed again and thought it terribly funny that the hemulen had had to do things he disliked all his life, only because he hadn't been able to put his foot down.

"Well, now, what *do* you want to do?" his maternal aunt asked cheerfully.

"I'd like to build myself a doll's house," the hemulen whispered. "The most beautiful doll's house in the world, with lots and lots of rooms, and all of them silent and solemn and empty."

Now the hemulens laughed so hard that they had to sit down. They gave each other enormous nudges and shouted: "A doll's house! Did you hear that! He said a doll's house!" and then they laughed themselves into tears and told him:

"Little dear, by all means do exactly as you like! You can have grandma's big park, very probably it's silent as a grave nowadays. That's the very place for you to rummage about in and play to your heart's content. Good luck to you, and hope you like it!"

"Thanks," the hemulen said, feeling a little shrunken inwardly. "I know you've always wished me well."

His dream about the doll's house with the calm and beautiful rooms vanished, the hemulens had laughed it to pieces. But it really was no fault of theirs. They would have felt sincerely sorry if anyone had told them that they had spoiled something for the hemulen. And it's a risky thing to talk about one's most secret dreams a bit too early.

The hemulen went along to grandma's old park that was now his own. He had the key in his pocket.

The park had been closed and never used since grandma had set fire to her house with fireworks and moved elsewhere with all her family.

That was long ago, and the hemulen was even a little uncertain about the way to the park.

The wood had grown, and ways and paths were under water. While he was splashing along the rain stopped as suddenly as it had started eight weeks ago. But the hemulen didn't notice it. He was wholly occupied with grieving over his lost dream and with feeling sorry because he didn't want to build a doll's house any more.

Now he could see the park wall. A little of it had tumbled down, but it was still quite a high wall. The single gate was rusty and very hard to unlock.

The hemulen went in and locked the gate behind him. Suddenly he forgot about the doll's house. It was the first time in his life that he had opened a door of his own and shut it behind him. He was home. He didn't live in someone else's house.

The rain clouds were slowly drifting away and the sun came out. The wet park was steaming and glittering all around him. It was green and unworried. No one had cut or trimmed or swept it for a very, very long time. Trees were reaching branches down to the ground, bushes were climbing the trees, and criss-crossing, in the luscious grass tinkled the brooks that grandma had led through the park in her time. They didn't take care of the watering any longer, they took care only of themselves, but many of the little bridges were still standing even if the garden paths had disappeared.

The hemulen threw himself headlong into the green, friendly silence, he made capers in it, he wallowed in it, and he felt younger than he ever had before.

Oh, how wonderful to be old and pensioned at last, he thought. How much I like my relatives! And now I needn't even think of them.

He went wading through the long, sparkling grass, he threw his arms around the trees, and finally he went to sleep in the sunshine in a clearing in the middle of the park. It was the place where grandma's house had been. Her great fireworks parties were finished long ago. Young trees were coming up all around him, and in grandma's bedroom grew an enormous rose-bush with a thousand red hips.

Night fell, lots of large stars came out, and the hemulen loved his park all the better. It was wide and mysterious, one could lose one's way in it and still be at home.

He wandered about for hours.

He found grandma's old fruit orchard where apples and pears lay strewn in the grass, and for a moment he thought: What a pity. I can't eat half of them. One ought to . . . And then he forgot the thought, enchanted by the loneliness of the silence.

He was the owner of the moonlight on the ground, he fell in love with the most beautiful of the trees, he made wreaths of leaves and hung them around his neck. During this first night he hardly had the heart to sleep at all.

In the morning the hemulen heard a tinkle from the old bell that still hung by the gate. He felt worried. Someone was outside and wanted to come in, someone wanted something from him. Silently he crept in under the bushes along the wall and waited without a word. The bell jangled again. The hemulen craned his neck and saw a very small whomper waiting outside the gate.

"Go away," the hemulen called anxiously. "This is private ground. I live here."

"I know," the small whomper replied. "The hemulens sent me here with some dinner for you."

"Oh, I see, that was kind of them," the hemulen replied willingly. He unlocked the gate and took the basket from the whomper. Then he shut the gate again. The whomper remained where he was for a while but didn't say anything.

"And how are you getting on?" the hemulen asked impatiently. He stood fidgeting and longed to be back in his park again.

"Badly," the whomper replied honestly. "We're in a bad way all of us. We who are small. We've got

no pleasure-ground any more. We're just grieving."

"Oh," the hemulen said, staring at his feet. He didn't want to be asked to think of dreary things, but he was so accustomed to listening that he couldn't go away either.

"You must be grieving, too," the whomper said with compassion. "You used to punch the tickets. But if one was very small and ragged and dirty you punched beside it. And we could use it two or three times."

"My eyesight wasn't so good," the hemulen explained. "They're waiting for you at home, aren't they?"

The whomper nodded but stayed on. He came

close to the gate and thrust his snout through it. "I must tell you," he whispered. "We've got a secret."

The hemulen made a gesture of fright, because he disliked other people's secrets and confidences. But the whomper continued excitedly:

"We've rescued nearly all of it. We keep it in the fillyjonk's barn. You can't believe how much we've worked. Rescued and rescued. We stole out at nights in the rain and pulled things out of the water and down from the trees and dried them and repaired them, and now it's nearly right!"

"What is?" asked the hemulen.

"The pleasure-ground of course!" the whomper cried. "Or as much of it as we could find, all the pieces there were left! Splendid, isn't it! Perhaps the hemulens will put it together again for us, and then you can come back and punch the tickets."

"Oh," the hemulen mumbled and put the basket on the ground.

"Fine, what! That made you blink," the whomper said. laughed, waved his hand and was off.

Next morning the hemulen was anxiously waiting by the gate, and when the whomper came with the dinner basket he called at once:

"Well? What did they say?"

"They didn't want to," the whomper said dejectedly. "They want to run a skating rink instead. And most of us go to sleep in winter, and anyway, where'd we get skates from . . ."

"That's too bad," the hemulen said, feeling quite relieved.

The whomper didn't reply, he was so disappointed. He just put down the basket and turned back.

Poor children, the hemulen thought for a moment. Well, well. And then he started to plan the leaf hut he was going to build on grandma's ruins.

The hemulen worked at his building all day and enjoyed himself tremendously. He stopped only when it was too dark to see anything, and then he went to sleep, tired and contented, and slept late the next morning.

When he went to the gate to fetch his food the whomper had been there already. On the basket lid he found a letter signed by several kiddies. "Dear pleasure-puncher," the hemulen read. "You can have all of it because you are all right, and perhaps you will let us play with you some time because we like you."

The hemulen didn't understand a word, but a horrible suspicion began burrowing in his stomach.

Then he saw. Outside the gate the kiddies had heaped all the things they had rescued from the pleasure-ground. It was a lot. Most of it was broken and tattered and wrongly re-assembled, and all of it looked strange. It was a lost and miscellaneous collection of boards, canvas, wire, paper and rusty iron. It was looking sadly and unexpectantly at the hemulen, and he looked back in a panic.

Then he fled into his park and started on his leaf hut again.

He worked and worked, but nothing went quite right. His thoughts were elsewhere, and suddenly the roof came down and the hut laid itself flat on the ground.

No, said the hemulen. I don't want to. I've only just learned to say no. I'm pensioned. I do what I like. Nothing else.

He said these things several times over, more and more menacingly. Then he rose to his feet, walked through the park, unlocked the gate and began to pull all the blessed junk and scrap inside.

*　　　　*　　　　*

The kiddies were sitting perched on the high wall around the hemulen's park. They resembled grey sparrows but were quite silent.

At times some one whispered: "What's he doing now?"

"Hush," said another. "He doesn't like to talk."

The hemulen had hung some lanterns and paper roses in the trees and turned all broken and ragged parts out of sight. Now he was assembling something that had once been a merry-go-round. The parts did not fit together very well, and half of them seemed to be missing.

"It's no use," he shouted crossly. "Can't you see? It's just a lot of scrap and nothing else! No!! I won't have any help from you."

A murmur of encouragement and sympathy was carried down from the wall, but not a word was heard.

The hemulen started to make the merry-go-round into a kind of house instead. He put the

horses in the grass and the swans in the brook, turned the rest up-side-down and worked with his hair on end. Doll's house! he thought bitterly. What it all comes to in the end is a lot of tinsel and gew-gaws on a dustheap, and a noise and racket like it's been all my life . . .

Then he looked up and shouted:

"What are you staring at? Run along to the hemulens and tell them I don't want any dinner tomorrow! Instead they might send me nails and a hammer and candles and ropes and some two-inch battens, and they'd better be quick about it."

The kiddies laughed and ran off.

"Didn't we tell him," the hemulens cried and slapped each other's backs. "He has to have something to do. The poor little thing's longing for his pleasure-ground."

And they sent him twice what he had asked for, and, furthermore, food for a week, and ten yards of red velvet, gold and silver paper in rolls, and a barrel organ just in case.

"No," said the hemulen. "No music box. Nothing that makes a noise."

"Of course not," the kiddies said and kept the barrel organ outside.

The hemulen worked, built and constructed. And while building he began to like the job, rather against his will. High in the trees thousands of mirror glass splinters glittered, swaying with the branches in the winds. In the treetops the hemulen made little benches and soft nests where people could sit and have a drink of juice without being observed, or just sleep. And from the strong branches hung the swings.

The roller coaster railway was difficult. It had to
be only a third of its former size, because so many
parts were missing. But the hemulen comforted
himself with the thought that no one could be
frightened enough to scream in it now. And from
the last stretch one was dumped in the brook, which
is great fun to most people.

But still the railway was a bit too much for the
hemulen to struggle with single-handed. When he
had got one side right the other side fell down, and
at last he shouted, very crossly:

"Lend me a hand, someone! I can't do ten things
at once all alone."

The kiddies jumped down from the wall and came
running.

After this they built it all jointly, and the hemulens sent them such lots of food that the kiddies were
able to stay all day in the park.

In the evening they went home, but by sunrise
they stood waiting at the gate. One morning they
had brought along the alligator on a string.

"Are you sure he'll keep quiet?" the hemulen
asked suspiciously.

"Quite sure," the whomper replied. "He won't
say a word. He's so quiet and friendly now that he's
got rid of his other heads."

One day the fillyjonk's son found the boa con-
strictor in the porcelain stove. As it behaved nicely
it was immediately brought along to grandma's
park.

Everybody collected strange things for the hemulen's pleasure-ground, or simply sent him cakes,

kettles, window curtains, toffee or whatever. It
became a fad to send along presents with the kiddies
in the mornings, and the hemulen accepted everything that didn't make a noise.

But he let no one inside the wall, except the
kiddies.

The park grew more and more fantastic. In the
middle of it the hemulen lived in the merry-go-
round house. It was gaudy and lopsided, resembling
most of all a large toffee paper bag that somebody
had crumpled up and thrown away.

Inside it grew the rosebush with all the red hips.

*   *   *

And one beautiful, mild evening all was finished.
It was definitely finished, and for one moment the
sadness of completion overtook the hemulen.

They had lighted the lanterns and stood looking
at their work.

Mirror glass, silver and gold gleamed in the great dark trees, everything was ready and waiting—the ponds, the boats, the tunnels, the switchback, the juice stand, the swings, the dart boards, the trees for climbing, the apple boxes . . .

"Here you are," the hemulen said. "Just remember that this is *not* a pleasure-ground, it's the Park of Silence."

The kiddies silently threw themselves into the enchantment they had helped to build. But the whomper turned and asked:

"And you won't mind that you've no tickets to punch?"

"No," said the hemulen. "I'd punch the air in any case."

He went into the merry-go-round and lighted the moon from the Miracle House. Then he stretched himself out in the fillyjonk's hammock and lay looking at the stars through a hole in the ceiling.

Outside all was silent. He could hear nothing except the nearest brook and the night wind.

Suddenly the hemulen felt anxious. He sat up, listening hard. Not a sound.

Perhaps they don't have any fun at all, he thought worriedly. Perhaps they're not *able* to have any fun without shouting their heads off . . . Perhaps they've gone home?

He took a leap up on Gaffsie's old chest of drawers and thrust his head out of a hole in the wall. No, they hadn't gone home. All the park was rustling and seething with a secret and happy life. He could hear a splash, a giggle, faint thuds and thumps,

padding feet everywhere. They *were* enjoying themselves.

Tomorrow, thought the hemulen, tomorrow I'll tell them they may laugh and possibly even hum a little if they feel like it. But not more than that. Absolutely not.

He climbed down and went back to his hammock. Very soon he was asleep and not worrying over anything.

*   *   *

Outside the wall, by the locked gate, the hemulen's uncle was standing. He looked through the bars but saw very little.

Doesn't sound as if they had much fun, he thought. But then, everyone has to make what he can out of life. And my poor relative always was a bit queer.

He took the barrel organ home with him because he had always loved music.

The Invisible Child

One dark and rainy evening the Moomin family sat around the verandah table picking over the day's mushroom harvest. The big table was covered with newspapers, and in the centre of it stood the lighted kerosene lamp. But the corners of the verandah were dark.

"My has been picking pepper spunk again," Moominpappa said. "Last year she collected flybane."

"Let's hope she takes to chanterelles next autumn," said Moominmamma. "Or at least to something not directly poisonous."

"Hope for the best and prepare for the worst," Little My observed with a chuckle.

They continued their work in peaceful silence.

Suddenly there were a few light taps on the glass

pane in the door, and without waiting for an answer Too-ticky came in and shook the rain off her oilskin jacket. Then she held the door open and called out in the dark: "Well, come along!"

"Whom are you bringing?" Moomintroll asked.

"It's Ninny," Too-ticky said. "Yes, her name's Ninny."

She still held the door open, waiting. No one came.

"Oh, well," Too-ticky said and shrugged her shoulders. "If she's too shy she'd better stay there for a while."

"She'll be drenched through," said Moomin-mamma.

"Perhaps that won't matter much when one's invisible," Too-ticky said and sat down by the table. The family stopped working and waited for an explanation.

"You all know, don't you, that if people are frightened very often, they sometimes become invisible," Too-ticky said and swallowed a small egg mushroom that looked like a little snowball. "Well. This Ninny was frightened the wrong way by a lady who had taken care of her without really liking her. I've met this lady, and she was horrid. Not the angry sort, you know, which would have been understandable. No, she was the icily ironical kind."

"What's ironical," Moomintroll asked.

"Well, imagine that you slip on a rotten mushroom and sit down on the basket of newly picked ones," Too-ticky said. "The natural thing for your mother would be to be angry. But no, she isn't.

Instead she says, very coldly: 'I understand that's your idea of a graceful dance, but I'd thank you not to do it in people's food.' Something like that."

"How unpleasant," Moomintroll said.

"Yes, isn't it," replied Too-ticky. "This was the way this lady used to talk. She was ironic all day long every day, and finally the kid started to turn pale and fade around the edges, and less and less was seen of her. Last Friday one couldn't catch sight of her at all. The lady gave her away to me and said she really couldn't take care of relatives she couldn't even see."

"And what did you do to the lady?" My asked with bulging eyes. "Did you bash her head?"

"That's of no use with the ironic sort," Too-ticky said. "I took Ninny home with me, of course. And now I've brought her here for you to make her visible again."

There was a slight pause. Only the rain was heard, rustling along over the verandah roof. Everybody stared at Too-ticky and thought for a while.

"Does she talk," Moominpappa asked.

"No. But the lady has hung a small silver bell around her neck so that one can hear where she is."

Too-ticky arose and opened the door again. "Ninny!" she called out in the dark.

The cool smell of autumn crept in from the garden, and a square of light threw itself on the wet grass. After a while there was a slight tinkle outside, rather hesitantly. The sound came up the steps and stopped. A bit above the floor a small silver bell was seen hanging in the air on a black ribbon. Ninny seemed to have a very thin neck.

"All right," Too-ticky said. "Now, here's your new family. They're a bit silly at times, but rather decent, largely speaking."

"Give the kid a chair," Moominpappa said. "Does she know how to pick mushrooms?"

"I really know nothing at all about Ninny," Too-ticky said. "I've only brought her here and told you what I know. Now I have a few other things to attend to. Please look in some day, won't

you, and let me know how you get along. Cheerio."

When Too-ticky had gone the family sat quite
silent, looking at the empty chair and the silver
bell. After a while one of the chanterelles slowly rose
from the heap on the table. Invisible paws picked it
clean from needles and earth. Then it was cut to
pieces, and the pieces drifted away and laid themselves in the basin. Another mushroom sailed up
from the table.

"Thrilling!" My said with awe. "Try to give her
something to eat. I'd like to know if you can see the
food when she swallows it."

"How on earth does one make her visible again,"
Moominpappa said worriedly. "Should we take her
to a doctor?"

"I don't think so," said Moominmamma. "I
believe she wants to be invisible for a while. Too-
ticky said she's shy. Better leave the kid alone until
something turns up."

And so it was decided.

The eastern attic room happened to be un-
occupied, so Moominmamma made Ninny a bed
there. The silver bell tinkled along after her upstairs
and reminded Moominmamma of the cat that once
had lived with them. At the bedside she laid out the
apple, the glass of juice and the three striped pieces
of candy everybody in the house was given at
bedtime.

Then she lighted a candle and said:

"Now have a good sleep, Ninny. Sleep as late as
you can. There'll be tea for you in the morning any
time you want. And if you happen to get a funny

feeling or if you want anything just come down-stairs and tinkle."

Moominmamma saw the quilt raise itself to form a very small mound. A dent appeared in the pillow. She went downstairs again to her own room and started looking through her Granny's old notes about Infallible Household Remedies. Evil Eye. Melancholy. Colds. No. There didn't seem to be anything suitable. Yes, there was. Towards the end of the notebook she found a few lines written down at the time when Granny's hand was already rather shaky. "If people start getting misty and difficult to see." Good. Moominmamma read the recipe, which was rather complicated, and started at once to mix the medicine for little Ninny.

★   ★   ★

The bell came tinkling downstairs, one step at a time, with a small pause between each step. Moom-introll had waited for it all morning. But the silver bell wasn't the exciting thing. That was the paws. Ninny's paws were coming down the steps. They were very small with anxiously bunched toes. Nothing else of Ninny was visible. It was very odd.

Moomintroll drew back behind the porcelain stove and stared bewitchedly at the paws that passed him on their way to the verandah. Now she served herself some tea. The cup was raised in the air and sank back again. She ate some bread and butter and marmalade. Then the cup and saucer drifted away to the kitchen, were washed and put away in the

closet. You see, Ninny was a very orderly little child.

Moomintroll rushed out in the garden and shouted: "Mamma! She's got paws! You can see her paws!"

I thought as much, Moominmamma was thinking where she sat high in the apple tree. Granny knew a thing or two. Now when the medicine starts to work we'll be on the right way.

"Splendid," said Moominpappa. "And better

still when she shows her snout one day. It makes me feel sad to talk with people who are invisible. And who never answer me."

"Hush, dear," Moominmamma said warningly. Ninny's paws were standing in the grass among the fallen apples.

"Hello Ninny," shouted My. "You've slept like a hog. When are you going to show your snout? You must look a fright if you've wanted to be invisible."

"Shut up," Moomintroll whispered, "she'll be hurt." He went running up to Ninny and said:

"Never mind My. She's hardboiled. You're really safe here among us. Don't even think about that horrid lady. She can't come here and take you away . . ."

In a moment Ninny's paws had faded away and become nearly indistinguishable from the grass.

"Darling, you're an ass," said Moominmamma. "You can't go about reminding the kid about those things. Now pick apples and don't talk rubbish."

They all picked apples.

After a while Ninny's paws became clearer again and climbed one of the trees.

It was a beautiful autumn morning. The shadows made one's snout a little chilly but the sunshine felt nearly like summer. Everything was wet from the night's rain, and all colours were strong and clear. When all the apples were picked or shaken down Moominpappa carried the biggest apple mincer out in the garden, and they started making apple-cheese.

Moomintroll turned the handle, Moominmamma fed the mincer with apples, and Moominpappa carried the filled jars to the verandah. Little My sat in a tree singing the Big Apple Song.

Suddenly there was a crash.

On the garden path appeared a large heap of apple-cheese, all prickly with glass splinters. Beside the heap one could see Ninny's paws, rapidly fading away.

"Oh," said Moominmamma. "That was the jar we use to give to the bumble-bees. Now we needn't carry it down to the field. And Granny always said that if you want the earth to grow something for you, then you have to give it a present in the autumn."

Ninny's paws appeared back again, and above them a pair of spindly legs came to view. Above the legs one could see the faint outline of a brown dress hem.

"I can see her legs!" cried Moomintroll.

"Congrats," said little My, looking down out of her tree. "Not bad. But the Groke knows why you must wear snuff-brown."

Moominmamma nodded to herself and sent a thought to her Granny and the medicine.

Ninny padded along after them all day. They became used to the tinkle and no longer thought Ninny very remarkable.

By evening they had nearly forgotten about her. But when everybody was in bed Moominmamma took out a rose-pink shawl of hers and made it into a little dress. When it was ready she carried it upstairs to the eastern attic room and cautiously laid it out on a chair. Then she made a broad hair ribbon out of the material left over.

Moominmamma was enjoying herself tremendously. It was exactly like sewing doll's clothes again. And the funny thing was that one didn't know if the doll had yellow or black hair.

*   *   *

The following day Ninny had her dress on. She was visible up to her neck, and when she came down to morning tea she bobbed and piped:

"Thank you all ever so much."

The family felt very embarrassed, and no one found anything to say. Also it was hard to know where to look when one talked to Ninny. Of course one tried to look a bit above the bell where Ninny was supposed to have her eyes. But then very easily one found oneself staring at some of the visible things further down instead, and it gave one an impolite feeling.

Moominpappa cleared his throat. "We're happy

to see," he started, "that we see more of Ninny today. The more we see the happier we are . . ."

My gave a laugh and banged the table with her spoon. "Fine that you've started talking," she said. "Hope you have anything to say. Do you know any good games?"

"No," Ninny piped. "But I've heard about games."

Moonintroll was delighted. He decided to teach Ninny all the games he knew.

After coffee all three of them went down to the river to play. Only Ninny turned out to be quite impossible. She bobbed and nodded and very seriously replied, quite, and how funny, and of

course, but it was clear to all that she played only from politeness and not to have fun.

"Run, run, can't you?" My cried. "Or can't you even jump?"

Ninny's thin legs dutifully ran and jumped. Then she stood still again with arms dangling. The empty dress neck over the bell was looking strangely helpless.

"D'you think anybody likes that?" My cried. "Haven't you any life in you? D'you want a biff on the nose?"

"Rather not," Ninny piped humbly.

"She can't play," mumbled Moomintroll.

"She can't get angry," little My said. "That's what's wrong with her. Listen, you," My continued and went close to Ninny with a menacing look. "You'll never have a face of your own until you've learned to fight. Believe me."

"Yes, of course," Ninny replied, cautiously backing away.

    ★   ★   ★

There was no further turn for the better.

At last they stopped trying to teach Ninny to play. She didn't like funny stories either. She never laughed at the right places. She never laughed at all, in fact. This had a depressing effect on the person who told the story. And she was left alone to herself.

Days went by, and Ninny was still without a face. They became accustomed to seeing her pink dress marching along behind Moominmamma. As soon

as Moominmamma stopped, the silver bell also stopped, and when she continued her way the bell began tinkling again. A bit above the dress a big rose-pink bow was bobbing in thin air.

Moominmamma continued to treat Ninny with Granny's medicine, but nothing further happened. So after some time she stopped the treatment, thinking that many people had managed all right before without a head, and besides perhaps Ninny wasn't very good-looking.

Now everyone could imagine for himself what she looked like, and this can often brighten up a relationship.

One day the family went off through the wood down to the beach. They were going to pull the boat up for winter. Ninny came tinkling behind as usual, but when they came in view of the sea she suddenly stopped. Then she lay down on her stomach in the sand and started to whine.

"What's come over Ninny? Is she frightened?" asked Moominpappa.

"Perhaps she hasn't seen the sea before," Moominmamma said. She stooped and exchanged a few whispering words with Ninny. Then she straightened up again and said:

"No, it's the first time. Ninny thinks the sea's too big."

"Of all the silly kids," little My started, but Moominmamma gave her a severe look and said: "Don't be a silly kid yourself. Now let's pull the boat ashore."

They went out on the landing-stage to the bathing

hut where Too-ticky lived, and knocked at the door.

"Hullo," Too-ticky said, "how's the invisible child?"

"There's only her snout left," Moominpappa replied. "At the moment she's a bit startled but it'll pass over. Can you lend us a hand with the boat?"

"Certainly," Too-ticky said.

While the boat was pulled ashore and turned keel upwards Ninny had padded down to the water's edge and was standing immobile on the wet sand. They left her alone.

Moominmamma sat down on the landing-stage and looked down into the water. "Dear me, how cold it looks," she said. And then she yawned a bit and added that nothing exciting had happened for weeks.

Moominpappa gave Moomintroll a wink, pulled a horrible face and started to steal up to Moomin-mamma from behind.

Of course he didn't really think of pushing her in the water as he had done many times when she was young. Perhaps he didn't even want to startle her, but just to amuse the kids a little.

But before he reached her a sharp cry was heard, a pink streak of lightning shot over the landing-stage, and Moominpappa let out a scream and dropped his hat into the water. Ninny had sunk her small invisible teeth in Moominpappa's tail, and they were sharp.

"Good work!" cried My. "I couldn't have done it better myself!"

Ninny was standing on the landing-stage. She had a small, snub-nosed, angry face below a red tangle of hair. She was hissing at Moominpappa like a cat.

"Don't you *dare* push her into the big horrible sea!" she cried.

"I see her, I see her!" shouted Moomintroll. "She's sweet!"

"Sweet my eye," said Moominpappa, inspecting his bitten tail. "She's the silliest, nastiest, badly-brought-uppest child I've ever seen, with or without a head."

He knelt down on the landing-stage and tried to fish for his hat with a stick. And in some mysterious way he managed to tip himself over, and tumbled in on his head.

He came up at once, standing safely on the bottom, with his snout above water and his ears filled with mud.

"Oh dear!" Ninny was shouting. "Oh, how great! Oh, how funny!"

The landing-stage shook with her laughter.

"I believe she's never laughed before," Too-ticky said wonderingly. "You seem to have changed her, she's even worse than little My. But the main thing is that one can see her, of course."

"It's all thanks to Granny," Moomin-mamma said.

The Secret of the Hattifatteners

Once upon a time, rather long ago, it so happened
that Moominpappa went away from home without
the least explanation and without even himself
understanding why he had to go.

Moominmamma said afterwards that he had
seemed odd for quite a time, but probably he hadn't
been odder than usual. That was just one of those
things one thinks up afterwards when one's bewildered and sad and wants the comfort of an
explanation.

No one was quite certain of the moment Moominpappa had left.

Snufkin said that he had intended to row out
with the hemulen to catch some alburn, but accord-
ing to the hemulen Moominpappa had only sat on

the verandah as usual and suddenly remarked that
the weather was hot and boring and that the landing-stage needed a bit of repair. In any case
Moominpappa hadn't repaired it, because it was as
lop-sided as before. Also the boat was still there.

So Moominpappa had set out on foot, and as he
could have chosen several directions there was no
point in looking for him.

"He'll be back in due time," Moominmamma
said. "That's what he used to tell me from the
beginning, and he always came back, so I suppose
he'll return this time too."

No one felt worried, and that was a good thing.
They had decided never to feel worried about each
other; in this way everybody was helped to a good
conscience and as much freedom as possible.

So Moominmamma started some new knitting
without making any fuss, and somewhere to the
west Moominpappa was wandering along with a
dim idea firmly in his head.

It had to do with a cape he once had seen on one
of the family picnics. The cape had pointed straight
out to sea, the sky had been yellow and a bit of
wind had sprung up towards night. He had never
been able to go out there to see what was on the

other side. The family wanted to turn home for tea.
They always wanted to go home at the wrong time.
But Moominpappa had stood on the beach for a
while, looking out over the water. And at that very
moment a row of small white boats with sprit sails
had come into sight under land, putting straight
out to sea.

"That's hattifatteners," the hemulen had said,
and in those words everything was expressed. A
little slightingly, a little cautiously, and quite
clearly with repudiation. Those were the outsiders,
half-dangerous, different.

And then an overpowering longing and melancholy had gripped Moominpappa, and the only
thing he knew for certain was that he didn't want
any tea on the verandah. Not that evening, nor any
other evening.

This had been quite a time ago, but the picture never left him. And so one afternoon he went away.

The day was hot, and he walked at random.

He didn't dare to think about it, nor to feel anything, he simply went on walking towards the sunset, screwing up his eyes under the hatbrim and whistling to himself, but no special tune. There were uphills and downhills, the trees came wandering towards and past him, and their shadows were beginning to lengthen.

At the moment when the sun dipped down into the sea Moominpappa came out on to the long gravel shore where no ways ever stopped and no one ever thought of going for a picnic.

He hadn't seen it before; it was a grey and dreary beach that told him nothing except that land ended and sea started here. Moominpappa stepped down to the water and looked outward.

And naturally—what else could indeed have happened?—at that very moment a little white boat came slowly gliding before the wind along the shore.

"Here they are," Moominpappa said calmly and started to wave.

There were only three hattifatteners aboard the boat. They were quite as white as the boat and the sail. One was sitting at the helm and two with their backs to the mast. All three were staring out to sea and looking as if they had been quarrelling. But Moominpappa had heard that hattifatteners never quarrel, they are very silent and interested only in travelling onwards, as far as possible. All the way to the horizon, or to the world's end, which is probably

the same thing. Or so people said. It was also said
that a hattifattener cared for nothing but himself,
and further that they all became electric in a
thunderstorm. Also that they were dangerous company to all who lived in drawing-rooms and
verandahs and were used to doing certain things at
certain times.

All this had greatly interested Moominpappa for
as long as he could remember, but as it isn't con-
sidered quite nice to talk about hattifatteners,
except indirectly, he still didn't know whether all
those things were true.

Now he felt a shiver from head to tail and in great
excitement saw the boat draw nearer. The hattifatteners did not signal to him in reply—one
couldn't even imagine them making such large
and everyday gestures—but it was quite clear that
they were coming for him. With a faint rustling
their boat ploughed into the gravel and lay still.

The hattifatteners turned their round, pale eyes
to Moominpappa. He tipped his hat and started to
explain. While he spoke the hattifatteners' paws
started to wave about in time to his words, and this
made Moominpappa perplexed. He suddenly found
himself hopelessly tangled up in a long sentence
about horizons, verandahs, freedom, and drinking
tea when one doesn't want any tea. At last he
stopped in embarrassment, and the hattifatteners'
paws stopped also.

Why don't they say anything? Moominpappa
thought nervously. Can't they hear me, or do they
think I'm silly?

He offered his paw and made a friendly, inter-rogatory noise, but the hattifatteners didn't move. Only their eyes slowly changed colour and became yellow as the evening sky.

Moominpappa drew his paw back and made a clumsy bow.

The hattifatteners at once rose and bowed in reply, very solemnly, all three at the same time.

"A pleasure," Moominpappa said.

He made no other effort to explain things, but clambered aboard and thrust off. The sky was burning yellow, exactly as it had been that other time. The boat started on a slow outward tack.

Never in his life Moominpappa had felt so at ease and pleased with everything. He found it splendid for a change not to have to say anything or explain anything, to himself or to others. He could simply sit looking at the horizon listening to the cluck of the water.

When the coast had disappeared a full moon rose, round and yellow over the sea. Never before had Moominpappa seen such a large and lonely moon. And never before had he grasped that the sea could be as absolute and enormous as he saw it now.

All at once he had a feeling, that the only real and convincing things in existence were the moon and the sea and the boat, with the three silent hattifatteners.

And the horizon, of course—the horizon in the distance where splendid adventures and nameless secrets were waiting for him, now that he was free at last.

He decided to become silent and mysterious, like a hattifattener. People respected one if one didn't talk. They believed that one knew a great many things and led a very exciting life.

Moominpappa looked at the hattifatteners at the helm. He felt like saying something chummy, something to show he understood. But then he let it alone. Anyway, he didn't find any words that—well, that would have sounded right.

What was it the Mymble had said about hatti-fatteners? Last spring, at dinner one day. That they led a wicked life. And Moominmamma had said: That's just talk: but My became enormously inter-ested and wanted to know what it meant. As far as Moominpappa could remember no one had been really able to describe what people did when they led a wicked life. Probably they behaved wildly and freely in a general way.

Moominmamma had said that she didn't even believe that a wicked life was any fun, but Moomin-pappa hadn't been quite sure. It's got something to do with electricity, the Mymble had said, cock-surely. And they're able to read people's thoughts, and that's not allowed. Then the talk had turned to other things.

Moominpappa gave the hattifatteners a quick look. They were waving their paws again. Oh, how horrible, he thought. Can it be that they're sitting there reading my thoughts with their paws? And now they're hurt, of course . . . He tried desperately to smooth out all his thoughts, clear them out of the way, forget all he had ever heard about

hattifatteners, but it wasn't easy. At the moment nothing else interested him. If he could only talk to them. It was such a good way to keep one from thinking.

And it was no use to leave the great dangerous thoughts aside and concentrate on the small and friendly sort. Because then the hattifatteners might think that they were mistaken and that he was only an ordinary verandah Moominpappa . . .

Moominpappa strained his eyes looking out over the sea towards a small black cliff that showed in the moonlight.

He tried to think quite simple thoughts: there's an island in the sea, the moon's directly above it, the moon's swimming in the water—coal-black, yellow, dark blue. At last he calmed down again, and the hattifatteners stopped their waving.

The island was very steep, although small.

Knobbly and dark it rose from the water, not very unlike the head of one of the larger sea-serpents.

"Do we land?" Moominpappa asked.

The hattifatteners didn't reply. They stepped ashore with the painter and made fast in a crevice. Without giving him a glance they started to climb up the shore. He could see them sniffing against the wind, and then bowing and waving in some deep conspiracy that left him outside.

"Never mind me," Moominpappa exclaimed in a hurt voice and clambered ashore. "But if I ask you if we're going to land, even if I see that we are, you might still give me a civil answer. Just a word or two, so I feel I've company."

But he said this only under his breath, and strictly to himself.

The cliff was steep and slippery. It was an unfriendly island that told everyone quite clearly to keep out. It had no flowers, no moss, nothing—it just thrust itself out of the water with an angry look.

All at once Moominpappa made a very strange and disagreeable discovery. The island was full of red spiders. They were quite small but innumerable, swarming over the black cliff like a live red carpet.

Not one of them was sitting still, everyone was rushing about for all his worth. The whole island seemed to be crawling in the moonlight.

It made Moominpappa feel quite weak.

He lifted his legs, he quickly rescued his tail and shook it thoroughly, he stared about him for a single spot empty of red spiders, but there was none.

"I don't want to tread on you," Moominpappa mumbled. "Dear me, why didn't I remain in the boat . . . They're too many, it's unnatural to be so many of the same kind . . . all of them exactly alike."

He looked helplessly for the hattifatteners and caught sight of their silhouettes against the moon, high up on the cliff. One of them had found something. Moominpappa couldn't see what it was.

No difference to him, anyway. He went back to the boat, shaking his paws like a cat. Some of the spiders had crawled on to him, and he thought it very unpleasant.

They soon found the painter also and started to crawl along it in a thin red procession, and from there further along the gunwale.

Moominpappa seated himself as far astern as possible.

This is something one dreams, he thought. And then one awakens with a jerk to tell Moominmamma: "You can't imagine how horrible, dearest, such a lot of spiders, you never . . ."

And she awakens too and replies: "Oh, poor Pappa—that was a dream, there aren't any spiders here . . ."

The hattifatteners were slowly returning.

Immediately every spider jumped high with fright, turned and ran back ashore along the painter.

The hattifatteners came aboard and pushed off. That boat glided out from the black shadow of the island, into the moonlight.

"Glory be that you're back." Moominpappa cried with great relief. "As a matter of fact I've never liked spiders that are too small to talk with. Did you find anything interesting?"

The hattifatteners gave him a long moon-yellow look and remained silent.

"I said did you find anything," Moominpappa repeated, a little red in the snout. "If it's a secret of course you can keep it to yourselves. But at least tell me there *was* something."

The hattifatteners were quite still and silent, only looking at him. At this Moominpappa felt his head grow hot and cried:

"Do you like spiders? Do you like them or not? I want to know at once!"

In the long ensuing silence one of the hattifatteners took a step forward and spread its paws.

Perhaps it had replied something—or else it was just a whisper from the wind.

"I'm sorry," Moominpappa said uncertainly, "I see." He felt that the hattifattener had explained to him that they had no special attitude to spiders. Or else it had deplored something that could not be helped. Perhaps the sad fact that a hattifattener and a Moominpappa will never be able to tell each other anything. Perhaps it was disappointed in Moominpappa and thought him rather childish. He sighed and gave them a downcast look. Now he could see what they had found. It was a small scroll of birch-bark, of the sort the sea likes to curl up and throw ashore. Nothing else. You can unroll them like documents: inside they're white and silk-smooth, and as soon as they're released they curl shut again. Exactly like a small fist clasped about a secret. Moominmamma used to keep one around the handle of her tea-kettle.

Probably this scroll contained some important message or other. But Moominpappa wasn't really curious any longer. He was a little cold, and curled up on the floor of the boat for a nap. The hatti-fatteners never felt any cold, only electricity

And they never slept.

Moominpappa awoke by dawn. He felt stiff in the back and still rather cold. From under his hatbrim he could see part of the gunwale and a grey triangle of sea falling and rising and falling again. He was feeling a little sick, and not at all like an adventurous Moomin.

One of the hattifatteners was sitting on the nearest thwart, and he observed it surreptitiously. Now its eyes were grey. The paws were very finely cut. They were flexing slowly, like the wings of a sitting moth. Perhaps the hattifattener was talking to its fellows, or just thinking. Its head was round and quite neckless. Most of all he resembles a long white sock, Moominpappa thought. A little frayed at the lower, open end, and as if made of white foam rubber.

Now he was feeling a little sicker still. He remembered his behaviour of last night. And those spiders. It was the first time he had seen a spider frightened.

"Dear, dear," Moominpappa mumbled. He was about to sit up, but then he caught sight of the birch-bark scroll and stiffened. He pricked his ears under the hat. The scroll lay in the bailer on the floor, slowly rolling with the movement of the boat.

Moominpappa forgot all about seasickness. His paw cautiously crept out. He gave the hattifatteners a quick look and saw that their eyes as usual were fixed on the horizon. Now he had the scroll, he closed his paw around it, he pulled it towards him. At that moment he felt a slight electric shock, no stronger than from a flashlight battery when you feel it with your tongue. But he hadn't been prepared for it.

He lay still for a long time, calming himself. Then started slowly to unroll the secret document. It turned out to be ordinary white birch-bark. No treasure map. No code letter. Nothing.

Perhaps it was just a kind of visiting card, politely left on every lone island by every hattifattener, to be found by other hattifatteners? Perhaps that little electric shock gave them the same friendly and sociable feeling one gets from a nice letter? Or perhaps they had an invisible writing unknown to ordinary trolls? Moominpappa disappointedly let the birch-bark curl itself back into a scroll again, and looked up.

The hattifatteners were regarding him calmly. Moominpappa reddened.

"We're all in the same boat, anyway," he said. And without expecting any reply he spread his paws like he had seen the hattifatteners do, in a helpless and regretful gesture, and sighed.

To this the wind replied with a faint howl in the tight stays. The sea was rolling grey waves all the way to the world's end, and Moominpappa thought with some sadness: If this is a wicked life I'd rather eat my hat.

*   *   *

There are many kinds of island, but all those that are small enough and far enough are without exception rather sad and lonesome. The winds chase all around them, the yellow moon increases

and wanes again, the sea becomes coal-black every night, but the islands are always unchanged, and only hattifatteners visit them now and then. They are not even real islands. They are skerries, rocks, reefs, forgotten streaks of land that perhaps even sink under water before daybreak and rise over the surface again during the night to take a look around. One can't know.

The hattifatteners visited them all. Sometimes a birch-bark scroll was there waiting for them. Sometimes there was nothing; the islet was just a smooth seal's back surrounded by breakers, or a ragged rock with high banks of red sea-weed. But on the summit of every island the hattifatteners left behind them a small white scroll.

They have an idea, Moominpappa thought. Something that's more important to them than all other matters. And I'm going to follow them about until I know what it is.

They met no more red spiders, but Moominpappa remained aboard every time they landed. Because those islands made him think of other islands far behind him, the picnic islands, the green and leafy bathing inlets, the tent, and the butter container cooling in the shadow by the boat, the juice glasses

in the sand, and the bathing-trunks adry on a sun-
hot boulder . . . Not that he missed that kind of
secure verandah life for a minute. Those were just
thoughts that came flapping past and made him a
bit sad. Thoughts about small and insignificant
things.

As a matter of fact Moominpappa had started to
think in a wholly new manner. Less and less often
he mused about things he had encountered in his
kindly and chequered life, and quite as seldom did
he dream about what his future would bring him.

His thoughts glided along like the boat, without
memories or dreams, they were like grey wandering
waves that didn't even want to reach the horizon.

Moominpappa stopped trying to talk to the
hattifatteners. He sat staring seawards, just as they
did, his eyes had turned pale like theirs, taking the
colour of the sky. And when new islands swam into
view he didn't even move, only tapped his tail once
or twice against the floor.

Once, as they glided along on the back of a slow,
tired swell, Moominpappa fleetingly thought: I
wonder if I'm beginning to resemble a hattifattener.

*   *   *

It had been a very hot day, and towards evening
a mist rolled in from the sea. It was a heavy,
curiously reddish mist. Moominpappa thought it
looked menacing and a little alive.

The sea-serpents were snorting and wallowing far

out, he could catch a glimpse of them at times. A round, dark head, startled eyes staring at the hattifatteners, then a splash from a tail fin and a quick flight back into the mist.

They're afraid like the spiders were, Moominpappa thought. Everyone's afraid of hattifatteners . . .

A far-away thunderclap went rolling through the silence, and everything was quiet and immobile once more.

Moominpappa always had thought thunderstorms very exciting. Now he didn't have any opinion about them. He was quite free, but he just didn't seem to have any likings any more.

At that moment a strange boat steered out of the mist with a large company aboard. Moominpappa jumped to his feet. In a moment he had become the old Moominpappa again, waving his hat about and shouting. The strange boat was coming straight

towards them. It was white, the sail was white. And the people aboard it were white . . .

"Oh, I see," Moominpappa said. He sat down again. The two boats continued their courses without exchanging any greeting.

And then one boat after the other glided out of the dark mist, all going the same way and all manned by hattifatteners. Sometimes by seven, sometimes by five, or eleven, at times even by one solitary hattifattener, but always by an odd number.

The mist cleared away and rolled into the slightly reddish evening dusk. The sea seemed to be packed with boats. All were on their way towards a new island, a low skerry with no trees and no high cliffs.

The thunder went rolling over again. It was hiding somewhere in the enormous black cloud that was now climbing higher and higher over the horizon.

One boat after the other put in and lowered sail. The lonely beach was already thronged by hattifatteners that had arrived earlier and were standing bowing to each other.

As far as one could see, white solemn beings were walking about and exchanging bows to right and left. They emitted a faint rustling sound and were constantly waving their paws. The beach grass whispered around them.

Moominpappa was standing aside by himself. He tried desperately to find his own hattifatteners among the crowd. He felt it to be important. They were the only ones he knew . . . slightly. Very slightly. But still.

They had disappeared in the throng, he could see no differences in the many hundreds of hattifatteners, and all at once Moominpappa was caught by the same terror as on the spider island. He pulled his hat down to his eyebrows and tried to look tough and at ease at the same time.

His hat was the only fixed and absolute thing on this strange island where all was white and whispering and vague.

Moominpappa didn't quite trust himself any longer, but he believed in his hat; it was black and resolute, and inside it Moominmamma had painted the words "M.P. from your M.M." to distinguish it from all other high hats in the world.

Now the last boat had landed and been pulled ashore, and the hattifatteners stopped rustling. They turned their reddish eyes towards Moominpappa, all together, and the next instant they began to move in his direction.

They want a fight, Moominpappa thought and was suddenly wide awake and rather elated. In that moment he felt like fighting anyone just to

fight and shout and feel sure that everyone else was wrong and deserving a good hiding.

Only hattifatteners never fight, nor do they object to anything or dislike anyone or hold any opinion at all.

They came to exchange bows with Moominpappa, all the hundreds of them, and Moominpappa tipped his hat and bowed in reply until he felt a headache coming on. Hundreds of paws waved at him until he also began waving his from sheer exhaustion.

When the last hattifattener had passed him Moominpappa had forgotten all about wanting a fight. His mind was polite and smooth, and he followed the others, hat in hand, through the whispering grass.

The thunderstorm had climbed high in the meantime and was hovering in the sky like a wall about to fall down. High up a wind was blowing, driving small rugged tufts of cloud before it in scared flight.

Close to the sea sudden and fitful lightning was flashing, switching off and flaring up again.

The hattifatteners had assembled in the centre of the island. They had turned southwards, where the thunderstorm waited, exactly like seabirds before a gale. One after the other they began to light up like little lamp bulbs, flaring in time with the lightning. The grass around them was crackling with electricity.

Moominpappa had laid himself on his back and was staring up at the pale green leaves around him.

Light, delicate leaves against a dark sky. In his easy-chair at home he had a cushion embroidered with fern leaves by Moominmamma. Pale green leaves against black felt. It was very beautiful.

The thunderstorm was nearing rapidly. Moominpappa felt faint shocks in his paws and sat up. There was rain in the air.

All of a sudden the hattifatteners began fluttering their paws like moth wings. They were all swaying, bowing and dancing, and a thin, gnat-like song arose from the lonely island. It was the howl of the hattifatteners, a lonely and yearning sound like wind in a bottleneck. Moominpappa felt an irresistible desire to do as the hattifatteners did. To sway back and forth, to sway and howl and rustle.

He felt a prickle in his ears, and his paws began to wave. He rose to his feet and started to walk towards the hattifatteners. Their secret's got to do with thunderstorms, he thought. It's thunderstorms they are always looking for and longing for . . .

Darkness fell over the island, and the lightning flashes were running straight down from the sky, like streams of dangerously white and hissing liquid. Far out the wind started to roar, and then the thunder broke loose, the fiercest thunder Moominpappa had ever experienced.

Heavy wagons of stone were rolling and rumbling back and forth, to and fro, and the wind caught hold of Moominpappa and threw him back in the grass.

He sat holding his hat and feeling the wind blow

through him, and all of a sudden he thought: No. What's come over me? I'm no hattifattener, I'm Moominpapa . . . What am I doing here?

He looked at the hattifatteners, and with electric simplicity he understood it all. He grasped that only a great thunderstorm could put some life in hattifatteners. They were heavily charged but hopelessly locked up. They didn't feel, they didn't think—they could only seek. Only in the presence of electricity they were able to live at last, strongly and with great and intense feelings.

That was what they longed for. Perhaps they were even able to attract a thunderstorm when they assembled in large crowds . . .

Yes, that must be the solution, Moominpappa thought. Poor hattifatteners. And I was sitting on my verandah believing they were so remarkable and free, just because they never spoke a word and were always on the move. They hadn't a single word to say and nowhere to go . . .

The skies opened and the rain crashed down, gleaming white in the flashes of lightning.

Moominpappa jumped to his feet. His eyes were as blue as ever, and he shouted:

"I'm going home! I'm leaving at once!"

He stuck his snout in the air and pulled his hat securely over his ears. Then he ran down to the beach, jumped aboard one of the white boats, hoisted sail and put straight out to the stormy sea.

He was himself once again, he had his own thoughts about things, and he longed to be home.

Just think, never to be glad nor disappointed, Moominpappa mused while the boat was carried along in the gale. Never to like anyone and get cross at him and forgive him. Never to sleep or feel

cold, never to make a mistake and have a belly-ache and be cured from it, never to have a birthday party, drink beer and have a bad conscience . . .

How terrible.

He felt happy and drenched and not in the least afraid of the thunderstorm. At home they would never have electric light, he decided, they'd keep the old kerosene lamps.

Moominpappa longed for his family and his verandah. All of a sudden he thought that at home he could be just as free and adventurous as a real pappa should be.

Cedric

Now, afterwards, it is hard to understand how that small beast, Sniff, could ever have been persuaded to give Cedric away.

Never before had Sniff done such a thing, rather the reverse. And furthermore Cedric really was quite wonderful.

Cedric wasn't alive, he was a thing—but what a thing! At first sight he was just a small plush dog, rather bald and love-worn, but a closer look showed that his eyes were nearly topazes and that he had a small genuine moonstone on his collar just beside the clasp.

And furthermore he carried an inimitable expression on his face, an expression that no other dog could ever have. Possibly the jewels were more important to Sniff than the expression, but in any case he loved Cedric.

And as soon as he had given Cedric away he

regretted it to desperation. He neither ate nor slept nor talked. He only regretted.

"But dearest Sniffy," Moominmamma said worriedly, "if you really did love Cedric so much, then why didn't you at least give him to someone you like and not to Gaffsie's daughter?"

"Pooh," Sniff mumbled, staring at the floor with his poor reddened eyes, "it was Moomintroll's fault. He told me that if one gives something away that one really likes, then one will get it back ten times over and feel wonderful afterwards. He tricked me to it."

"Oh," Moominmamma said. "Well, well." She didn't find anything better to say. She felt she had to sleep on the matter.

Evening fell, and Moominmamma went to bed. Everybody said good night, and the lights were put

out, one after the other. Only Sniff lay awake, staring up at the ceiling, where the shadow of a large branch was moving up and down in the moonlight. Through the open window he could hear Snufkin's mouth organ playing in the warm night down by the river.

When Sniff's thoughts became too black he jumped out of bed and padded to the window. He climbed down the rope ladder and ran through the garden where the peonies gleamed white and all the shadows were coal-black. The moon was high, far away and impersonal.

Snufkin was sitting outside his tent.

He didn't play any complete tunes tonight, only small shreds of music that resembled questions or those small concurring sounds one makes when one doesn't know what to say.

Sniff sat down beside him and looked disconsolately into the river.

"Hullo," Snufkin said. "Good thing you came. I've been sitting here thinking about a story that might interest you."

"I'm not interested in fairy tales tonight," Sniff mumbled, wrinkling himself up.

"It's no fairy tale," Snufkin said. "It's happened. It happened to an aunt of my mother's."

And Snufkin started his story, sucking at his pipe and now and then splashing with his toes in the dark river water.

*   *   *

"Once upon a time there was a lady who loved all her belongings. She had no children to amuse or annoy her, she didn't need to work or cook, she didn't mind what people said about her, and she wasn't the scared sort. Also she had lost her taste for play. In other words, she found life a bit boring."

"But she loved her beautiful things and she had collected them all her life, sorted them and polished them and made them more and more beautiful to look at. One really didn't believe one's eyes when one entered her house."

"She was a happy lady," Sniff nodded. "What kinds of things did she have?"

"Well," Snufkin said. "She was as happy as she knew how to be. And now don't interrupt me, please. Then, one night it happened that this aunt of my mother's went down to her dark scullery to

eat a cold cutlet, and she swallowed a large bone. She felt funny for several days afterwards, and when she didn't get any better she went to her doctor. He tapped her chest and listened to it and X-rayed her and shook her about, and at last he told her that this cutlet bone had stuck crosswise somewhere inside her. It was impossible to prise it loose. In other words, he feared the worst."

"You don't say," Sniff said, showing a little more interest in the story. "He thought the lady was going to kick the bucket but he didn't dare tell her?"

"That's about it," Snufkin agreed. "But this aunt of my mother's wasn't easily scared, so she made him tell her how much time she had left, and then she went home to think. A few weeks wasn't very much."

"She suddenly remembered that in her youth she had wanted to explore the Amazonas, to learn deep sea diving, to build a large nice house for lonely children, to see a volcano, and to arrange a gigantic party for all her friends. But all that was too late now, of course. Friends she had none at all, because she had only collected beautiful things, and that takes time."

"She grew more and more sad while she wandered around in her rooms. Her wonderful belongings gave her no comfort. On the contrary, they only made her think of the day when she'd go to heaven and leave them all behind her."

"And the thought of starting a new collection up there didn't make her at all happy, whatever the reason."

"Poor lady!" Sniff cried. "Couldn't she take the least little thing along with her?"

"No," Snufkin said. "It's not allowed. But now dry up, please, and listen. One night this aunt of my mother's lay awake looking up in the ceiling and brooding. All around her stood lots of beautiful furniture, and all over it were lots of beautiful knick-knacks. Her things were everywhere, on the floor, on the walls, on the ceiling, in her cabinets, in her drawers—and suddenly she felt about to suffocate among all those belongings that gave her no comfort at all. And now an idea came to her. It was such a funny idea that this aunt of my mother's began to laugh where she lay. All at once she was feeling fit, and she rose and dressed and started to think."

"She had hit upon the idea to give away everything she owned. That would give her more breathing space, and it's something you need if you've a large bone stuck in your stomach and want to be able to think of the Amazonas."

"How silly," Sniff said disappointedly.

"It wasn't silly in the least," Snufkin objected. "She had lots of fun while she sat thinking out what things to give away to whom."

"She had many relations and knew still more people, you see, that's quite possible even if you've no friends. Well, she thought of everyone, one after the other, and wondered what he or she would like best. It was like a game."

"And she wasn't stupid. To me she gave the mouth organ: Perhaps you haven't known it's gold

and rosewood? Well. She thought it out so wisely that everybody got exactly the thing that suited him and that he had dreamt of."

"This aunt of my mother's also had a turn for surprises. She sent all the things in parcels, and the receivers had no idea of who the sender was (they had never been in her home, because she had always been afraid they'd break things)."

"It amused her to imagine their astonishment, their thoughts and guesses, and she was feeling quite superior. A little like those fairies that fulfil wishes in a jiffy as they fly along."

"But I didn't send Cedric in a parcel," Sniff cried with bulging eyes. "And I'm not going to die either!"

Snufkin sighed. "You're the same as ever," he
said. "But still, try to listen to a good story, can't you,
even if it isn't about yourself. And think of me a bit,
too. I've saved this story for you, and sometimes I
like telling stories. Well, all right. At the same time
something else was happening. This aunt of my
mother's suddenly found that she was able to sleep
at nights, and in the daytime she dreamed of the
Amazonas and read books on deep sea diving and
drew plans for that house for children no one
wanted. She had fun, and that made herself nicer
than usual, and people began to like her company.
I must beware, she thought. Before I know a word
I'll have a lot of friends and no time to arrange that
enormous party I've dreamed about . . ."

"Her rooms were becoming airier and airier. She
sent off one parcel after the other, and the fewer
possessions she had left, the lighter she felt. Finally,
she was walking about in empty rooms, feeling
rather like a balloon, a happy balloon ready to
fly away . . ."

"To heaven," Sniff observed drily. "Now,
listen . . ."

"Don't interrupt me all the time," Snufkin said.
"I can hear you're too small for this story. But I'm
going to finish it anyway. Good. By and by all her
rooms were empty, and this aunt of my mother's
had only her bed left."

"It was a large canopied bed, and when her new
friends came to visit her it could hold them all, and
the smallest ones sat up in the canopy. Everybody
had a wonderful time, and her only worry was about

that great party which she didn't seem to find the time to have."

"They used to tell ghost stories and funny stories all the night, and then one evening . . ."

"I know, I know," Sniff said crossly. "You're exactly like Moomintroll. I know how it turned out. Then one evening she gave away her bed too and then she went off to heaven and was *so* happy, and the right thing for me to do is to give away not only Cedric but everything I have and then hand in my spade and bucket on top of it all!"

"You're an ass," Snufkin said. "Or, still worse, you're a spoil-story. What I was about to relate was how this aunt of my mother's laughed so terribly at one of the funny stories, that the bone jumped out of her stomach and she became absolutely well!"

"You don't say," Sniff cried, "the poor lady!"

"How do you mean, the poor lady," Snufkin asked.

"Don't you see! She had given all her things away, hadn't she," Sniff cried. "Quite uselessly! Because she didn't die after all! Did she take all her things back then?"

Snufkin bit hard at his pipe and raised his eyebrows.

"You foolish little beast," he said. "She made the whole thing into a funny story. And then she gave a party. And built the house for lonely children. She was too old for deep sea diving, but she saw the volcano. And then she went off to the Amazonas. That was the last we heard about her."

"Such things cost money," Sniff said with

practical disbelief. "She had given everything away, hadn't she?"

"Had she? Indeed?" Snufkin replied. "If you'd have listened as you should you'd remember that she kept the canopied bed, and this bed, my dear Sniff, was made of gold and simply crammed with diamonds and carneoles."

(As for Cedric, Gaffsie made the topazes into eardrops for her daughter and gave Cedric black button eyes instead. One day Sniff found him lying forgotten in the rain and took him back home. The rain had washed away the moonstone which was never found again. But Sniff went on loving Cedric all the same, even if he now did it only for love's sake. And this does him some honour, I believe. AUTHOR'S NOTE)

The Fir Tree

One of the hemulens was standing on the roof, scratching at the snow. He had yellow woollen mittens that after a while became wet and disagreeable. He laid them on the chimney top, sighed and scratched away again. At last he found the hatch in the roof.

That's it, the hemulen said. And down there they're lying fast asleep. Sleeping and sleeping and sleeping. While other people work themselves silly just because Christmas is coming.

He was standing on the hatch, and as he couldn't remember whether it opened inwards or outwards he stamped on it, cautiously. It opened inwards at once, and the hemulen went tumbling down among snow and darkness and all the things the Moomin family had stowed away in the attic for later use.

The hemulen was now very annoyed and further-more not quite sure of where he had left his yellow mittens. They were his favourite pair.

So he stumped down the stairs, threw the door open with a bang and shouted in a cross voice: "Christmas's coming! I'm tired of you and your sleeping and now Christmas will be here almost any day!"

The Moomin family was hibernating in the draw-ing-room as they were wont to do. They had been sleeping for a few months already and were going to keep it up until spring. A sweet sleep had rocked them through what felt like a single long summer afternoon. Now all at once a cold draught disturbed Moomintroll's dreams. And someone was pulling at his quilt and shouting that he was tired and Christmas was coming.

"Is it spring already?" Moomintroll mumbled.

"Spring?" the hemulen said nervously. "I'm talking about Christmas, don't you know, Christ-mas. And I've made absolutely no arrangements yet myself and here they send me off to dig you out. I believe I've lost my mittens. Everybody's running about like mad and nothing's ready . . ."

The hemulen clumped upstairs again and went out through the hatch.

"Mamma, wake up," Moomintroll said anxi-ously. "Something's on. They call it Christmas."

"What d'you mean?" his mother said and thrust her snout out from under her quilt.

"I don't really know," her son replied. "But nothing seems to be ready, and something's got lost, and all are running about like mad. Perhaps there's a flood again."

He cautiously shook the Snork Maiden by the shoulder and whispered: "Don't be afraid, but something terrible's happening."

"Eh," Moominpappa said. "Easy now."

He rose and wound the clock that had stopped somewhere in October.

Then they followed the hemulen's wet trail upstairs and climbed out on to the roof of the Moominhouse.

The sky was blue as usual, so this time it couldn't be the volcano. But all the valley was filled with wet cotton, the mountains and the trees and the river and the roof. And the weather was cold, much colder than in April.

"Is this the egg whites?" Moominpappa asked wonderingly. He scooped up some of the cotton in his paw and peered at it. "I wonder if it's grown out of the ground," he said. "Or fallen down from the sky. If it came all at the same time that must have been most unpleasant."

"But Pappa, it's snow," Moomintroll said. "I know it is, and it doesn't fall all at the same time."

"No?" Moominpappa said. "Unpleasant all the same."

The hemulen's aunt passed by the house with a fir tree on her chair-sledge.

"So you're awake at last," she observed casually. "Better get yourself a fir before dark."

"But why," Moominpappa started to reply.

"I haven't time now," the hemulen's aunt called

back over her shoulder and quickly disappeared.

"Before dark, she said," the Snork Maiden whispered. "The danger comes by dark, then."

"And you need a fir tree for protection," Moominpappa mused. "I don't understand it."

"Nor I," Moominmamma said submissively. "Put some woollen socks and scarfs on when you go for the fir. I'll make a good fire in the stove."

*   *   *

Even if disaster was coming Moominpappa decided not to take one of his own firs, because he was particular about them. Instead he and Moomintroll climbed over Gaffsie's fence and chose a big fir she couldn't very well have any use for.

"Is the idea to hide oneself in it?" Moomintroll wondered.

"I don't know," Moominpappa said and swung his axe. "I don't understand a thing."

They were almost by the river on their way back when Gaffsie came running towards them with a lot of parcels and paper bags in her arms.

She was red in the face and highly excited, so she did not recognize her fir tree, glory be.

"What a mill, what a fuss it all is!" Gaffsie cried. "Badly brought-up hedgehogs should never be *allowed* to . . . And as I've told Misabel, it's a shame . . ."

"The fir," Moominpappa said, desperately clinging to Gaffsie's fur collar. "What does one *do* with one's fir?"

"Fir," Gaffsie repeated confusedly. "Fir? Oh, what a bother! Oh, how horrid . . . I haven't dressed mine yet . . . how on earth can I find the time . . ."

She dropped several parcels in the snow, her cap slipped askew and she was near to tears from pure nervousness.

Moominpappa shook his head and took hold of the fir again.

*   *   *

At home Moominmamma had dug out the verandah with a shovel and laid out life-belts, aspirin, Moominpappa's old gun and some warm compresses. One had to be prepared.

A small woody was sitting on the outermost edge
of the sofa, with a cup of tea in its paws. It had been
sitting in the snow below the verandah, looking so
miserable that Moominmamma had invited it in.

"Well, here's the fir," Moominpappa said. "If
we only knew how to use it. Gaffsie said it had to be
dressed."

"We haven't anything large enough," Moominmamma said worriedly. "Whatever did she mean?"

"What a beautiful fir," the small woody cried and
swallowed some tea the wrong way from pure
shyness, regretting already that it had dared to speak.

"Do *you* know how to dress a fir tree?" the Snork
Maiden asked.

The woody reddened violently and whispered:
"In beautiful things. As beautifully as you can. So
I've heard." Then, overwhelmed by it's shyness, it
clapped its paws to its face, upset the teacup and
disappeared through the verandah door.

"Now keep quiet a moment, please, and let me
think," Moominpappa said. "If the fir tree is to be
dressed as beautifully as possible, then it can't be
for the purpose of hiding in it. The idea must be to
placate the danger in some way. I'm beginning to
understand."

They carried the fir out in the garden and planted
it firmly in the snow. Then they started to decorate
it all over with all the most beautiful things they
could think up.

They adorned it with the big shells from the
summertime flowerbeds, and with the Snork
Maiden's shell necklace. They took the prisms from

the drawing-room chandelier and hung them from the branches, and at the very top they pinned a red silk rose that Moominpappa had once upon a time given Moominmamma as a present.

Everybody brought the most beautiful thing he had to placate the incomprehensible powers of winter.

When the fir tree was dressed the hemulen's aunt passed by again with her chair-sledge. She was steering the other way now, and her hurry was still greater.

"Look at our fir tree," Moomintroll called to her.

"Dear me," said the hemulen's aunt. "But then you've always been a bit unlike other people. Now I must . . . I haven't the least bit of food ready for Christmas yet."

"Food for Christmas," Moomintroll repeated. "Does he eat?"

The aunt never listened to him. "You don't get away with less than a dinner at the very least," she said nervously and went whizzing down the slope.

Moominmamma worked all afternoon. A little before dark she had the food cooked for Christmas,

and served in small bowls around the fir tree. There was juice and yoghurt and blueberry pie and eggnog and other things the Moomin family liked.

"Do you think Christmas is very hungry?" Moominmamma wondered, a little anxiously.

"No worse than I, very likely," Moominpappa said longingly. He was sitting in the snow with his quilt around his ears, feeling a cold coming on. But small creatures always have to be very, very polite to the great powers of nature.

Down in the valley all windows were lighting up. Candles were lit under the trees and in every nest among the branches, and flickering candle flames went hurrying through the snowdrifts. Moomintroll gave his father a questioning look.

"Yes," Moominpappa said and nodded. "Preparing for all eventualities." And Moomintroll went into the house and collected all the candles he could find.

He planted them in the snow around the fir tree and cautiously lighted them, one after one, until all were burning in a little circle to placate the darkness and Christmas. After a while everything seemed to quieten down in the valley; probably everyone had gone home to await what was coming. One single lonely shadow was wandering among the trees. It was the hemulen.

"Hello," Moomintroll called softly. "Is he coming?"

"Don't disturb me," the hemulen replied sullenly, looking through a long list in which nearly every line seemed to be crossed out.

He sat down by one of the candles and started to count on his fingers. "Mother, Father, Gaffsie," he mumbled. "The cousins . . . the eldest hedgehog . . . I can leave out the small ones. And Sniff gave me nothing last year. Then Misabel and Whomper, and auntie, of course . . . This drives me mad."

"What is it?" the Snork Maiden asked anxiously. "Has anything happened to them?"

"Presents," the hemulen exclaimed. "More and more presents every time Christmas comes around!"

He scribbled a shaky cross on his list and ambled off.

"Wait!" Moomintroll shouted. "Please explain . . . And your mittens . . ."

But the hemulen disappeared in the dark, like all the others that had been in a hurry, and beside themselves over the coming of Christmas.

So the Moomin family quickly went in to look for some presents. Moominpappa chose his best trolling-spoon which had a very beautiful box. He wrote "For Christmas" on the box and laid it out in the snow. The Snork Maiden took off her ankle ring and sighed a little as she rolled it up in silk paper.

Moominmamma opened her secret drawer and took our her book of paintings, the one and only coloured book in all the valley.

Moomintroll's present was so lavish and private that he showed it to no one. Not even afterwards, in the spring, did he tell anyone what he had given away.

Then they all sat down in the snow again and waited for the frightening guest.

Time passed, and nothing happened.

Only the small woody who had upset the cup of tea appeared from behind the woodshed. It had brought all its relations and the friends of these relations. Everyone was as small and grey and miserable and frozen.

"Merry Christmas," the woody whispered shyly.

"You're the first to say some such thing," Moomin-pappa said. "Aren't you at all afraid of what's going to happen when Christmas comes?"

"This is it," the woody mumbled and sat down in the snow with its relations. "May we look? You've got such a wonderful fir tree."

"And all the food," one of the relations said dreamingly.

"And real presents," said another.

"I've dreamed all my life of seeing this at close quarters," the woody said with a sigh.

There was a pause. The candles burned steadily in the quiet night. The woody and its relations were sitting quite still. One could feel their admiration and longing, stronger and stronger, and finally Moominmamma edged a little closer to Moomin-pappa and whispered: "Don't you think so too?"

"Why, yes, but if . . . ," Moominpappa objected.

"No matter," Moomintroll said. "If Christmas gets angry we can close the doors and perhaps we'll be safe inside."

Then he turned to the woody and said: "You can have it all."

The woody didn't believe its ears at first. It stepped cautiously nearer to the fir tree, followed by

all the relations and friends with devoutly quivering whiskers.

They had never had a Christmas of their own before.

"I think we'd better be off now," Moominpappa said anxiously.

They padded back to the verandah, locked the door and hid under the table.

Nothing happened.

After a while they looked anxiously out of the window.

All the small creatures were sitting around the fir tree, eating and drinking and opening parcels and have more fun than ever. Finally they climbed the fir and made fast the burning candles on the branches.

"Only there ought to be a star at the top," the woody's uncle said.

"Do you think so?" the woody replied, looking thoughtfully at Moominmamma's red silk rose. "What difference does it make once the idea's right?"

"The rose should have been a star," Moominmamma whispered to the others. "But how on earth?"

They looked at the sky, black and distant but unbelievably full of stars, a thousand times more than in summer. And the biggest one was hanging exactly above the top of their fir tree.

"I'm sleepy," Moominmamma said. "I'm really too tired to wonder about the meaning of all this. But it seems to have come off all right."

"At least I'm not afraid of Christmas any more,"

Moomintroll said. "I believe the hemulen and his aunt and Gaffsie must have misunderstood the whole thing."

They laid the hemulen's yellow mittens on the verandah rail where he'd be sure to catch sight of them, and then they went back to the drawing-room to sleep some more, waiting for the spring.

A suspenseful mystery with a surprise ending!

THE CHRISTMAS TREE MYSTERY

by Wylly Folk St. John

Beth Carlton was in trouble. She accused Pete Abel of steal-
ing the Christmas ornaments from her family tree, something
she knew he hadn't done. And what was worse—the police
believed her! Beth had two days to prove to the police that
Pete wasn't a thief, and all she had to go on was her step-
brother's word that Pete was innocent.

An Avon Camelot Book
30569 $1.25

Avon Camelot Books are available at your bookstore. Or, you may use Avon's
special mail order service. Please state the title and code number and send with
your check or money order for the full price, plus 50¢ per copy to cover postage
and handling, to: AVON BOOKS, Mail Order Department, 250 West 55th Street,
New York, New York 10019. Please allow 4-6 weeks for delivery.